MEMORIES AND IMAGININGS

*An Anthology of Creative
Writing in Late Life*

Christine Colyar
Bonnie Cotton
Jean Gant Delastrada
Dan Jorgensen
Martha Iles Worcester
Barbara Mould Young

Dedicated to Keith Eisner, Writing Instructor, who brought us together, and inspired us to keep writing.

CONTENTS

Title Page
Dedication
Authors   1
Introduction   3
Christine Colyar   5
The Unforgettable Feast   6
Christmas Cookie Day   9
Life Has Become a Meaningful Book of Poetry   11
Heartwood   13
Feathers   18
Ravioli Tuscano   19
Whispered Wings   23
Bonnie Cotton   26
Life in the second person   27
Home Place   31
Dying Well   39
Jean Gant Delastrada   50
Outliers   51
Downloading Success   53
Bad Genes and Robots   61

Trapped	70
Save As	74
Dan Jorgensen	76
Francis	77
Father's Day	84
Dear Sidne	87
One Day at the Home	90
Martha Iles Worcester	94
Call Me Mr. Grump!	95
Softening Sorrow	98
Maggie and Mr. Charles	106
Candle	115
Barbara Mould Young	117
Depois da Hors do Urubu	118
Emily and Alfahad	122
Purple Ruffles #Me Too	125
Dream Time: "Here Lies Son of a Bitch"	130
Prayers	133
Let	136
Beethoven, Chopin, Joplin	138
Dia De Los Muertos	141
Friend in Care Home	143
Christine Colyar	148
Bonnie Cotton	149
Jean Cook Stickney	151
Dan Jorgensen	152
Martha iles Worcester	153
Barbara Mould Young	155

AUTHORS

## 1	Christine Colyar

TRUTH AND POSSIBILITIES
The Unforgettable Feast
Christmas Cookie Day
Life Has Become A Meaningful Book Of Poetry
Heartwood
Feathers
Ravioli Tucano
Whispered Wings

## 2	Bonnie Cotton

LIFE HAPPENS: A POEM AND TWO ESSAYS
Life in the second person
Home Place
Dying Well

## 3	Jean Gant Delastrada

STORIES OF DIFFERENCES
Outliers
Downloading Success

Bad Genes and Robots
Trapped
Save As

4   Dan Jorgensen

STORIES, A MEMORY, AND A LETTER
Francis
Father's Day
Dear Sidne
One Day at the Home

5   Martha Iles Worcester

CONNECTING OLD AND YOUNG
Call me Mr. Grump!
 Softening Sorrow
 Maggie and Mr. Charles
 Candle

6   Barbara Mould Young

STORIES THROUGH TIME
Depois da Hora Do Uburu
   (After the Hour of the Vulture)
Purple Ruffles, #Me Too
Dream Time: "Here Lies Son of a Bitch"
Prayers
Let
Beethoven, Chopin, Joplin
Dia De Los Muertos (Day of the Dead)
Friend in Care Home

INTRODUCTION

Within these pages, you will find a collection of writings: personal narrative, professional reflections, fiction, creative nonfiction, memoir, fantasy, and a bit of poetry. What we six, "beyond middle-aged" (actually senior citizens) hold in common, is the experience of writing under the tutelage and instruction of Keith Eisner, at the Senior Services for South Sound Center in Olympia, Washington

Between 2015 and 2017, we accepted the challenge of writing eight to ten pages per week, responded to prompts for subject matter, completed exercises introducing different genres, and acquired skills of critique and group accountability. We are grateful to Keith for his good nature and gentle coaching throughout the two years of his "Beautiful Lies, Beautiful Truths" classes. Our writing improved and we committed to continue writing, relying on our writer's gathering for useful feedback and encouragement.

Keith and subsequent instructors (Olivia Archibald, Jim Lynch, and others) each encouraged us to join or create writing circles to enhance our writing, stay on task, focus, and offer support and useful criticism to one another.

At the time of printing our ages range from 71 to 81. We share this collection of our writing as a means of encouragement to others as old or older than we are, believing the wealth of our experiences and acquired knowledge may inspire others to take the opportunity to engage in this means of expression. What you will see on these pages is our product, not the process of writing.

Our backgrounds are in the fields of nursing (Barbara and Martha), teaching (Christine) and counseling (Jean), pastoral ministry (Bonnie), and construction (Dan). For five years we have shared our lives as well as our writing. Births of grandchildren, deaths of loved ones, the beginning, and ending of partnerships, celebrations of new marriages, as well as shared ideologies and political leanings, have given us insights into why we write what we write. We gather monthly to connect and critique, encouraging improvement and submission of our work for possible publication.

CHRISTINE COLYAR

Truth and Possibilities

THE UNFORGETTABLE FEAST

FOR ME, IT IS A THRILL to come downstairs early Sunday morning, the family still snoozing, and find the federalist dining table strewn with surviving debris of last night's dinner party. I walk the table's perimeter between the harp-back chairs and collect foils and corks, wine-stained glasses, and linen napkins —some neatly folded and others forming random peaks and mountain ranges down the length of the table. Prying the overflowing candle wax off my favorite jacquard linen tablecloth with a paring knife feels somewhat like reading Uncle Meade's diary finding he has a secret crush on our sister-in-law, Mavis. A little like trespassing.

I read the dinner table remains—the blue fountain pen, the small stack of artichoke leaves, one silver cuff link—as if they are relics of the chat, the secrets, the cherished conversations just hours earlier: records of conversations I always miss while in the kitchen dishing up billowing baked Alaska.

Inspecting the remains, I suspect while reciting a few lines of poetry, the Champagne cage twists into the shape of a butterfly. The chocolate truffle papers become origami jumping frogs while the conversation turns to the subject of deciphering the mind of a difficult daughter-in-law. I clear and polish that table, and I loosely catalog all the tangible things people arrange and rearrange while conversing, listening, and concluding at dinner party conversations.

To me, it is always clear that a dinner party is about what is said, not what is eaten. There is always merlot and Mediterranean salad and Yorkshire pudding, beef bourguignon, chocolate mousse, and cucumber citrus-infused sparkling water. But those are just the props that become the path for funny and honest and meaningful conversations; the required parts of a lively, engaged, lingering dinner party, the one I always chase.

Memories of the first dinner party in my small college apartment are delightful. After shopping, prepping, cooking, and setting the table with unmatched silverware and china, I recall arranging a wildflower centerpiece. Even before completing our salads, I remember us announcing our future plans and travels, university, and creative adventures. Thinking back, I was bold as well as naive while suggesting a future well beyond my level of experience.

Still, I carry on spending any extra money on French drinking glasses, wild-caught salmon, rib steaks, crab legs, and fresh greens, Spode china, silver place settings, and branches for arranging down the centers of tables.

Always a couple of guests know exactly what to do. They on no occasion come too early but allow you a 10-minute breather just past arrival time. They never just plop their paper-wrapped lily bouquet on the kitchen prep counter in the middle of your work, but instinctively look in the likely locations for a vase and arrange those flowers, trash the wrappings, leaving your counters clean, and securing your friendship forever. When less experienced guests arrive, those perfect friends guide them quickly to the bedroom to stash their coats and bags so they won't sling them over the backs of chairs at the dinner table I spent hours arranging. Over the next 30 years, those couple of perfect friends grow to be many. I find comfort in a gathering of kindred spirits and an evening of precious conversations. The dripping of candles continues as we sit, eat, drink, talk, tell jokes, argue, and talk more. And the wine glasses, bottles, foils and corks, and even baguette heals on the table I curiously interpret the next morning.

I am against the demanding, well-meaning cleanup crew that gathers in the kitchen before anybody has even digested.

Those people who push back their chairs and clear dessert might miss the calm when I dip my finger in the wine and circle it around the rim of my wineglass to make tones like those from a monastery in Sri Lanka. When I invite you over, I mean it. Sit down. I take care of you. I clean up. And when I come to your house, I am 10 minutes late with a bottle, my conversation, good mood, and appetite. It is the greatest thing of all time.

When guests arrive with their phones, we stop looking at one another across the table as images take the place of our words. As our words diminish, people find it challenging to express their feelings. The room empties of stories or engaging conversations. As photos are snapped images replace rich and enchanting talk.

I persevere and delight in creating these precious moments. The dinner party depends on having one frequently. The guest collection only includes those who enrich the conversation and therefore the lives of each other. There is always a well-set table and wine and cucumber and lemon-infused sparkling water and another perfect friend, and then yet another. I always invite some outliers, some unexpecteds. Set the table. Arrange the chairs and the centerpiece of wild things and light all the candles—it will make it all just right. Creating a piece of unforgettable.

CHRISTMAS COOKIE DAY

PICTURE A MORNING IN EARLY DECEMBER. It is a welcoming-of-winter morning we reenact each year. Consider a cottage in the forest whose garden is asleep beneath Winter's cold, dreaming of distant blooms. Within the small warm kitchen is a heated black stove, butter softening on the counter, and chilled heavy cream at the ready to transform into truffles lightly dusted with Dutch Chocolate Powder. On a long dining table are large glass jars and biscuit tins, lids off, waiting to be filled with sweet goodness.

Christine leads this endeavor of Christmas Cookie Day. Her thick grey hair held back with a polka-dot scarf, wooden spoon in hand, she stands in the kitchen above a large crock mixing bowl. She wears wool slippers, blue jeans, and red linen apron, with big pockets stuffed with her collection of recipes. Tall and lively—she is the conductor of a sugared symphony.

Then there is Barney who, this very morning, claims to be her newly assigned assistant. His task is making pizzeles, which require the perfect heating of a special iron notched with beautiful snowflake designs. He meets the challenge of this task with the artistic grace of a cookie engineer.

This is that time of year when visions of Christmas past drift in and out of memory like the gently falling snow. We remember when Longfellow quotes assisted in the making of snow-covered tree cards engraved with, 'soft and silent and slow descends the snow'. Ornaments hand made with each grandchild's photo transforming them into snowmen, elves, and gatherers of shells and flowers. Brown craft paper stockings on the mantle we stitch together with a cheerful ruffle at the top. We plan a lavish brunch for 14 favorite people accompanied by piano duets, singing, laughing, and storytelling.

People come and go, but their cheerful faces around the large dining table passing the feast always remain in our memories. One part of Christmas is forever the same: Christmas Cookie Day.

It occurs every year in this house; it is a continuing tradition. Christmas baking memories continue with grandmother's Pecan Balls, Uncle Mo's Mince Meat with secret ingredients, and Mother's powdered sugar dusted Date Nut Bars. Favorite recipes from the past include changes to improve the magic mixtures.

We make Cranberry Walnut Oatmeal Bars, Gingerbread, Whipped Shortbread, Cream Cheese Orange and Lemon Bars, Fudge, and Peanut Brittle. We prepare, individually wrap, and store in jars and tins until Christmas Eve morning when we stuff a little bit of everything into ruffle-trimmed paper stockings. All the sweetness we deliver to porches this year. It is a year of Pandemic when we must celebrate together apart. This year, this Christmas Eve morning, we pack all of the stuffed stockings in a large picnic basket, warm up the car, and set off on our adventure. Those who would have come to Christmas Eve brunch receive their Christmas stocking with porch deliveries filled with the smell of Christmas and the ringing of bells.

LIFE HAS BECOME A MEANINGFUL BOOK OF POETRY

UNFURL LAYERS OF QUILTS AND BLANKETS IN THE DARK, come down the stairs into the living room, and tie back the front window curtains. While sitting in the soft leather chair, spend the next early morning hour writing, reading, and being in the quiet stillness of the start of this day. As the room slowly lightens, like an empty stage set, realize morning is the loveliest most hopeful time. Be aware, this day is another play in which, you, again, are the playwright. With pen in hand and artistic license, write the script, and the dialogue, develop the main characters and manage the props.

A life story of caring for children now focuses on your own life, without the requirements of parenthood. The house is no longer the set to rock babies, make peanut butter cookies for school parties, or being forced awake at 1 in the morning waiting for the night to return the teenager who hopefully had been made ready for independence under your tutelage. In those days, joy, terror, and immense patience chased each other through the hallways.

Life is simple now.

It was about soccer games, music performances, and the Pythagorean theorem. There are only memories of the hand-built volcanoes prepared for eruption, searching once again for the elusive pet gerbil, and boom boxes playing unintelligible sounds. The props also have become still lives: glass candlesticks, poetry books, and a wooden bowl filled with bananas.

It is quiet now. Life has become a meaningful book of poetry. Life does not happen anymore; you are the director who makes it happen.

There is no burden to create each day from scratch, for you are not responsible for anybody but yourself. Gaze about the house full of paintings and paintbrushes, quilts and fabrics, books and bookcases. It seems like too much stuff for a one-woman play. Imagine clearing out the extras, and moving to a tiny house. Then you think again. You are not quite ready for the gypsy's life.

Considerations are made of letting go of those things that are not important to the plot while trying not to complicate it with people or tasks that divert your attention too far off the path. Unless, of course, it is a marvelous four-day visit with the granddaughters.

Everyone needs friends their own age, but nobody likes to be locked into a single focus, and Bailey and Kiley, who are twin 7-year old's, make sure that does not happen. For four days the house becomes a play within a play where props are used with abandon and everything sparkles. You gasp as they rearrange and help themselves to all of the candlesticks and vases with a promise not to peek. You prepare for a tea party with each candle lit and forever memories are made of this moment. Every time when you invite them back, you think they will not want to come again, but every time they do. This includes Monopoly property investments, blackberry tart baking, giggling, and storytelling. Kiley says, "Let's do this until we are thirty." You agree and are silently amused at what that might look like.

After stories by flashlight, we welcome sleep. You had forgotten the sweetness of your home filled with sleeping children. You tiptoe down the stairs to sit by the fire as you used to do when their dad was sleeping down the hall. You savor the reliving of that lovely time in your life when all the beds were full. Then you pull the curtains shut across the living room window, and close down the show for the night.

HEARTWOOD

AS I TOOK A ROADTRIP through the back intersections of my life after so long a time, always the memories of the cherry tree were brightest. Imagine a backyard cherry tree planted by the builder of a simple two-story Southern Gothic-style house. It was a three-foot sapling he found beside a winding dirt road —the seed dropped perhaps from the beak of a cedar waxwing some two years earlier. Expecting it to grow into a very tall and broad tree, he carefully chose a place not so close to the home that it would keep the morning light from entering the shuttered windows of the breakfast nook, but far enough away to allow the limbs to grow as intended, broad and strong. And, there it was planted, the sweet cherry tree, Prunus avium. It was a self-pollinator with abundant blooms in the spring, producing fragrant pink flowers. After pollination, the tree developed small red fruit. It grew to 40 feet under full sun in moist and acidic soil.

The tree grew as the inhabitants of that home also grew. The builder was a shipwright by trade and began as a journeyman at the age of 17, having many opportunities as a Merchant Marine traveling to exotic and curious places. But, home was strongest on his compass. He was my father's uncle and his name was Ira Colyar. Home from sea and yearning to leave the rhythm of the tides, Ira built a fine two-story home with a cellar beneath. He built it on a bluff in the seaside town of Port Townsend. The sea was always in view from the tall turret window and the sure and steady land was safe beneath his feet.

As a shipwright, Ira built and repaired boats and ships of all sizes. Shipwrights design and build ships according to the specifications of individuals or companies. Depending on the size of the ship, he used hand and power tools to construct the vessel himself or oversaw a team of shipbuilders. Ira was secure in the fact that he could build anything.

Imagine that backyard cherry tree planted when the simple house was built more than eighty years ago. The tree grew taller than the river stone chimney. The strength of its limbs and the circumference of its trunk showed its age while the paint on the house revealed the toll of weather and time. This tree offered reliable cherries in the spring for pies and strudel and cobbler, jam, and tarts. It made a canopy for family and neighborly picnics in its big shade during the summer sun. Known by cousins, uncles, and an occasional adventurous auntie as the best climbing tree, its branches were positioned in just the right places like the rungs of the orchard's ladder. All welcomed the chance to dream of a place beyond home. When the climb started, there was no stopping curiosity until the top was reached. The view from that perch was splendid indeed of salt water, ferry boats, and gently rolling hills, railroad tracks, and a green suspension bridge. I imagined destinations beyond that horizon and the thoughts of people and what sort of stories they told. On the descent, I observed but did not disturb, robin nests and a solitary beehive.

When I found the day unbearably warm and without a chance of breeze in the forecast, I sat on the double seated swing hanging from the strongest branch. It was a double swing, with room enough for two. We often called it the kissing swing for many a relationship began there while floating above ground.

For those in need of less adventure, there was the cozy treehouse built with cousins one summer of scrap wood found here and there. We climbed inside by the open window with book or journal and created our own story. Also known as the Henny Penny Garrison from which I tossed many cherries on the heads of unsuspecting postmen or neighbors, and just once on the head of the formidable Father Milner who came calling to demand more money for the church.

Yes, this cherry tree was a big part of my life. I expected it to provide its strength and beauty and cherries forever. But, one night in October there was a wild and roaring storm, the kind of storm that makes you imagine Dorothy's adventure in the land of Oz. Well, unfortunately, that storm chose to strike my beloved cherry tree. The lightning hit it with a crack. The tree split right down the middle falling to the ground with a thud. I was sad and without words. Grandad noticed the heartwood in the center of the tree was exceptionally large. My cherry tree had a very large heart; it enriched my life and made my heart big too. While Dad suggested cutting up the tree for firewood, Grandad preferred putting it in the barn to cure while deciding on a more fitting purpose.

And, there it sat until my family grew with new sons-in-law and daughters-in-law and babies, and, at family dinners, the dining table seemed to get smaller and smaller.

Uncle Bill said, "Why don't I build us a table out of that old lightning tree in the barn?" Being his father's son, he could build anything. And so, he did. He sawed and sanded and measured and marveled at the size of its heart and very soon he had a table ready for the inaugural dinner. That cherry tree had so much more to give my family.

The legs were beautifully shaped and connected with a trestle near the floor. The table could be small to seat four or made larger to seat eight or twelve. Every morning began at that table eating oatmeal before leaving for school or Dad's delicious hash browns and jelly omelets on Sunday mornings.

Everything began and ended at that big-hearted cherry wood table. Think about the kitchen of any old house in any small town. Of course, there was a stove, sink, and refrigerator, but there was also a big table with chairs placed around it. That table was at the center of our lives. That table was filled with those beginning their day with breakfast and conversation about last night's stories and today's possibilities.

Plans began here and life changes were made in conversation. We gossiped, recalled enemies and the ghosts of lovers. We laughed and cried, planned and wished. At this table, we sang with joy, with sadness, and we wrote new lyrics for a new tomorrow. We prayed for healing and we gave thanks. We told our stories. The conversation was bold and intelligent and angry, sometimes unwanted and filled with fear. We shared difficult decisions. It was where we made funeral plans for my father and arranged flowers for my son's wedding. Where we solved the world's problems and family problems. It is where my son announced he would like to get married in the backyard. It was a place to be nurtured or forbidden to be real.

Feasts for family and friends were shared at this table and prepared here. For the yearly Chinese New Year Dim Sum, guests were busy at the table rolling eggrolls and crimping pot stickers, and writing fun fortunes for the fortune cookies. Harvested gifts from the garden were shared at this table.

The pasta machine was cranked and fettuccini was left to dry to become Pasta Alfredo. Egg beaters whirled in bowls of butter and sugar on birthday mornings baking your favorite cake to celebrate the day. I lit the candles when guests came from far away for dinner or from next door.

It is here that children learned what it means to be human. We created plans to stitch a peace quilt for the people of Israel and Palestine. I sewed my wedding dress at that table and deliberated my divorce there. My daughter and I built dulcimers at the table and played them one Mother's Day for a church performance. Many quilts were constructed there: Log Cabin, Dresden Plate and Ohio Star.

It's where I wrote stories of my life, and my history, and visualized a future at this table.

Uncle Bill noticed something in the long straight grain of that old cherry tree. He called it the Heartwood. The table will always be the place to gather. It has been since the beginning, and it will go on. Dogs savor the crumbs under it. Babies teeth at the corners. This table has been a tent, a house, and a hiding place where we are hoping to be found. We fell apart at this table and put ourselves back together.

We announced our next child's birth at this table. It was

a desk, an ironing board, and a game table where we played monopoly, poker, and dominoes.

I covered that table with a fine cotton or linen cloth and set it for dinner guests. Other times paper covered the table for the craft group's creations of collages or flea market candlesticks. And during times when I missed that climb to view horizons, I did not cover the table, but I admired the beauty in the heart of that tree, the tree that has brought to me the heart of humanity.

Today, it is a long table with no one at the other end. And on Thursdays, it is where the book club meets for a lively conversation about everything. And where I light a candle in memory of the friend who is here in spirit.

It can seat four, six, eight, or twelve. It is adjustable just like me.

FEATHERS

EVERY WEDNESDAY AT 7 PM he sits in a tan folding lawn chair listening to music in the park. This week it's samba and tango. He sits alone, his chair separate while surrounded by groups of family and friends eating picnics, dancing, and laughing. He is expressionless while his eyes are on the musicians. His whole body is still, not even a foot or finger taps to the lively beat of the music. He wears khaki cuffed slacks, brown loafers, and dark green checked shirt he has ironed crisp with creases down each short sleeve, topped off with a navy-blue cap. As he begins to chew on a fingernail he pulls a clipper from his right pocket for trimming. I find him sitting on the same square of grass each Wednesday, alone, among friends and families.

This day becomes a glorious day to bond with one small part of humanity. He is silent and makes no welcoming gesture, but he is chosen. He is the one preferred among many possibilities. Is it the emptiness in his eyes? Is it an intuitive need fulfilled?

A toddler approaches the man from the family blanket nearby carrying a small white seagull feather. He drops it to slowly float to the grass and excitedly captures it again. Eyes meet as he hands the feather to the man sitting alone among this crowd. Both become animated, giggling, delighted in the moment of a feather's gift. Young and old touching the compassion of each heart.

He remembers that small child with the floating feather late into the evening at his nightly visit while tucking his love into bed. As the disease consumes her present, she becomes more of her past. Calling her husband Papa, and yearning for permission, remembering to ask again, to ride her bike to the park to gather seagull feathers.

RAVIOLI TUSCANO

I LIVE ITALIAN IN NAPA VALLEY for a two-week vacation every summer with my Nona Emma. She has a table in the outdoor summer kitchen dedicated to only rolling pasta. Her hair is freshly braided and arranged in a large circle on her head resembling a halo-like in the come to Jesus paintings in her bedroom. Little frizzles of hair frame her sweet face. An apron is always worn over her calico dress, and this morning the pink chenille slippers we gave her for Christmas are on her already tired feet. The only other shoes she wears are those black thick-heeled lace-up grandma shoes for church and shopping for sales at the K Mart.

I am ten and as the ravioli-making begins, I ask how I can help. All she says is no. Nona Emma refuses to speak English since her arrival in America for a marriage arranged by her parents when she was only nineteen. The Ellis Island documentation I found states she is in good health, has twenty-four dollars for a train trip to San Francisco, and her brother will meet her at her destination. I am not allowed to help, but I am allowed to watch. I am wishing today that I had taken photos with my Dad's Argosy camera to help my memory of 65 years. Some vivid pictures always remain. After she mixes the flour and egg with her hands in the middle of that table, she rolls the translucent dough, then folds it into thirds, sprinkles on some flour, and rolls it again. Flour is everywhere: flour in her hair, flour on the floor, and flour somewhat suspended through the filtered summer sunlight entering the window. She does this rolling and folding seven times, one of her many superstitions she rails about, including broken mirrors and open umbrellas inside the house, black cats, and walking under ladders.

At the end of her seventh rolling, Nona Emma presses her ravioli rolling pin into the thin sheet of dough to mark the squares. With a curved knife, she chops and mixes the filling in a large wooden bowl. Swiss chard is included as well as garlic, ricotta and beef brains from my uncle's butcher shop. After placing a small amount of filling in each square, another sheet of pasta blankets over the top. Pressing the rolling pin over again seals each little pillow of goodness. Ravioli falls gently into the boiling water for three minutes until al dente. When I ask for a taste of one ravioli, Nona Emma's smile confirms her appreciation of my excitement. The pasta melts in my mouth while the filling explodes with flavors. Our precious time together adds to the amazing taste of that ravioli.

We put the red and white checked tablecloth on the table and I arrange the plates, forks, knives, and spoons. The uncles, aunties, and cousins arrive with their hugs and laughter. Nona Emma presents the oval white platter piled with ravioli and steaming red sauce. She grins with pride at everyone's 'delizioso.' The tender, melt-in-your-mouth texture of the pasta and the rich flavors of the sauce is unforgettable all these years later. There is always salad with olive oil and red wine vinegar, sourdough garlic bread, and always angel food cake for dessert topped with strawberries and whipped cream. We eat until past full while Nona Emma insists that we eat even more. "Mangia, Mangia."

That long dinner table filled with Italian relatives stays in my memory, everyone laughing and talking loudly at the same time, arms moving, cheek kissing, wine toasting, and yelling. Sometimes I hide under the table in fear they are arguing, but, no, they are Italian!

When dinner is over and all the dishes left on the table, my grandfather, Nono Michalino, makes his announcement. I never anticipate what is next, but it happens every time there is a large family dinner at Nona Emma's and Nono Michalino's house.

Nono Michalino is ragged around the edges, to say the least. He is not a cozy huggable old man and all his teeth are tobacco stained. He is bald except for prickly white whiskers bordering his chin and his face is nearly the same color and texture as the walnut shells on the trees in the yard with deep crevices and wrinkles. He makes wine in the garage and asphyxiates the extra kittens in a cardboard box with the car exhaust. While the grandchildren watch, he shoots robins with his B B gun and eats them for lunch.

Nono Michalino, the husband of this arranged marriage, every Wednesday polishes the fifteen-year-old light brown Pontiac coupe and vacuums the wool mohair seats where he lays a ribboned bouquet of swiss chard, carrots, and roses. He is flitting about excited as a schoolboy going to his first dance, for on Wednesday evenings he packs up his casserole and dresses up in his crisp white shirt and tie and freshly polished brogans to attend the Sons of Italy potluck and dance. The aunties speak only in whispers about the unimaginable cavorting with other women while Nona Emma says two extra rosaries to keep him safe from any possible attachments! He deserves the fear and disgust we feel for him, and I am convinced that if his physical features do not allow him charm or handsomeness, then he has chosen to be the best at grotesque.

So, when he announces, "I will remove the table cloth and not break one dish." He creates a magical moment, and I know that in that instant my disdain for this hunched-back grizzly character is suspended. While he takes such a chance, he transforms before me from monster to honorable magician. Aunties insist we remove wine glasses while Nona Emma begs him not to be so "stupido." Nono Michalino insists with confidence, "No, I can do this." And, every time, he is right! And every time, we expect disaster and a trip to the city to buy new dishes in the morning. In fact, aunties tell Nona Emma about the wonderful new dishes she might have to choose from. Every dish, fork, and knife remains on the table -- in its same location. Nono Michalino loves the spectacle and the proof that yes, only he can do this, once again.

When I tell my Uncle Tootie that I learned to make ravioli

today, he says, "You learned to make ravioli? You know it takes brains!"

WHISPERED WINGS

IT WAS A CRISP BLUE-SKY SUMMER MORNING when I heard the slow turning of rusty wheels in my backyard. There had been a noisy roadwork crew nearby, and I assumed that caused the commotion. I opened the back door to hundreds of starlings perched in fir trees mimicking the sounds of the road crew's equipment. Amazing birds! Memories flooded back some sixty years before of my Grandmother's voice and many stories she shared. Gram told me of Mozart who had purchased a starling he discovered in a pet shop. He was immediately attracted to it as it sang out the third movement of his Piano Concerto No. 17 in G, which Mozart had recently played in a public park where he often performed his new works.

Starlings had roosted near her farm since she could remember. Gram was especially attracted to starlings because they have the ability to mimic sounds in their environment: music, sirens, other birds, machines, and even Gram's voice.

Gram showed me a painting of Mozart's Starling sitting on his shoulder as he composed. It assisted him by singing back his tunes, often rearranging the parts. Mozart was captivated by his bird who became another musician with whom he could share ideas. Because the starling appeared to have many white stars on its feathers, Mozart named him Vogel Staar which translates to Bird Star. Vogel Staar was his constant companion for thirty-six months. When the starling suddenly died, Mozart wrote a funeral poem for burial in his backyard. He invited twelve guests who wore black masks with yellow beaks. Mozart's father had died a week earlier with no funeral.

Gram always had a story. She was a collector of feathers, bird nests, houses, perches, and feeders. She always said a feather is a letter from a bird. On my eleventh birthday, this generous and soulful woman added a starling surprise to my day. It was almost dusk and just past supper when Gram told me the Starlings had a special gift for me. Gram and I went in search of what she called murmurations.

Memories come back to me so clearly after all these years. The trees were still and leafless and the sky was glowing with what was left of the day's light. The mist was settling in the fields and wind gently kissed our cheeks. Somewhere behind us, a foghorn sounded, long and low, like a promise or surrender. I could hear it through the cap Gram had pulled over my ears. A tugboat answered the foghorn, and then a coyote howled. They spoke to each other in the mist, in the cold, at the end of day. When the sounds quieted it was as hushed as a snowflake. We walked on silently toward the fields.

Our footprints in the frozen snow assured me that we would find our way back home. Gram held my mittened hand and the other was kept warm in my woolen pocket. It was too dim for shadows and cold enough to see our breath. Through the forest, we could see low bushes and green distant fields. Gram pointed to a small group of starlings. These birds were shiny and iridescent with little white specks on their feathers, just like Vogel Staar. They moved slowly with a waddle like a duck, appearing big and clumsy. They looked like my winter starlight quilt. I said, "Hello beautiful, hello starlight."

Gram looked up as if searching for something. We found a low log to perch on where we waited. The silence and beauty and crisp cold surrounded us like a blanket of dreams. Then we walked on. I felt the cold on my nose while the rest of me was warm.

We traveled through a small forest making our own trail between the dark trees. I moved slowly between fear and bravery as I wondered what lived behind those dark trees in the coming night. Then we came to a clearing. The moon was bright and hanging just above us. The snow reflected in moonlight as bright as the ten candles on my birthday cake.

Then it happened. Nothing on that meadow moved. Then, quiet wingbeats of 500 Starlings lifted upward sounding like a starling's secret whisper. They moved together, dropped into shallow ponds, then lifted again to form curved and moving shapes in the sky. They were graceful and moving in unison, making an oval, spiraling into a whirling tornado and crescent. These acrobats in crisp cold air were dipping and floating in all directions. The performance was in the sky above the meadow. I looked so hard my eyes filled with tears. How did they know when to turn and swoop?

Then, all of a sudden, the starlings flew right over us. Gram hugged me tight, our cheeks sandwiched together, our eyes on the dance, the rhythm of the dance in the sky, blessing us with their splendid flight. Then, they came back to their roost. We stared at one another for a second or ten minutes. Those little starred birds dancing for me lifted off their perches like a mysterious shadow one more time. The only sound was the air against their feathers. Lovely, gentle, and full of a gift of kindness. Gram smiled; I smiled too. It was as if she and the starlings had arranged this most magnificent performance for me, just for my birthday.

As Gram said it was time to go home, I knew then I could talk, but I was as quiet as a cloud as we walked home. Remembering the rhythm of the dance and the quiet and Gram's warm hand in mine. We heard a voice from the nearby trees, "Hello beautiful, hello starlight." Amazing birds!

When you go in search of murmurations you need patience, a love of beauty, and gratitude that soars on whispered wings.

BONNIE COTTON

Life Happens:
A poem and two essays

LIFE IN THE SECOND PERSON

YOU BEGIN in an act of passion
    it is warm and dark
    nourished by your mother's life
    sharing heartbeats
    Until
     muscles push you into a world of light and sound and cold.

You cry
Your needs are simple
    crying brings food
    or comfort when you are wet
    or cold or full of gas,
You learn
    loving hands will bring
    relief or change.

You hear the voice you knew from the beginning
You copy the sounds you hear
    and see others smile,
    your smile brings praise and kisses and laughter;
    you repeat sounds that become names
    of people and things that fill your world.
You practice words.

You wiggle and explore
    legs and arms work in tandem
    you roll from front to back, laughing
    you discover

    knees lift you off your belly
    you rock and scoot backward
    Until
    you find yourself moving forward.

You crawl
    You raise your arms
        someone lifts you up
    they hold your hands while you stand
    you lift one foot after the other,
    move toward outstretched arms
    You are eager for the rewarding hug
You learn to walk.

You alternate between walking and running
    the world gets larger still
    comes with warnings
    " Hot! Don't touch!"
    " Slow down!"
    " Be careful! "
    "Wait for Mommy!"

You go to school
    You learn letters and numbers
    how to share and take turns.
You think new thoughts
    ask new questions
    discover another gender
    identify your own
    you test the limits and break the rules,
    trusting parents, teachers, preachers,
    and community to keep you safe.

You believe
    life is good
        people are kind
       you are loved

Until…
someone bullies you or lies to you or disappoints
    your heart is broken
You grow a protective shield
learn to doubt.

You explore your body,
    touching where you find pleasure
    yearning for another's touch,
    to give pleasure in return.
You hold tight, tremble,
    then let go, trying to be pure,
    to "remember who you are,"
        to do what you've been told is right
    Until
    Passion turns to love
    and mutual desire.

You give your heart.
You commit your life and love to another.
You believe the future will unfold as planned,
    with two kids and a dog
    Until
    the day comes
    you experience the greatest loss.

You want to die along with love.

You swallow tears, repress your anger,
    practice patience,
    take risks,
    try your luck,
    gather courage,
    gain resilience,
    express opinions,
    experience outrage,
        find your compass,

   dream new dreams
   live with faith,
   embrace hope.

Over time you remember
All in all
Love prevails.

(Exercise in writing in the second person for Keith Eisner's class, "Beautiful Lies, Beautiful Truths," 2017)

HOME PLACE

ON MY 72ND BIRTHDAY, I wake before the sun rises. The bombardier squirrels knock cones off the fir trees, aiming them at the metal roof above my head. The intermittent tap, tap, tap of the woodpecker seeking grubs from the tree outside the window adds to my annoyance and delight. Two stellar jays argue over the territory where we have supplied peanuts. I slip out of bed, leaving my sleeping family undisturbed. Walking into the main room of our family cabin, I turn toward the wall of windows facing the lake. The monochromatic pastels of dawn begin to deepen. The mystical moment of light reaching over the edge of Bead Lake Peak to color the earth draws me outside. It is a warm July morning, yet I grab the afghan from the couch on my way. Looking directly east, yellow light adds brilliance to the air. The water is smooth as glass, without a ripple. There are no clouds, no breeze, nothing but the rich green of cedar, pine, and fir trees, the brown and gray rocks along the shoreline, and the deep blue water swallowing the lighter blue sky. A line of sunlight stretches across the water, reflecting the sun cresting the hill.

I am not a morning person, except here. Here my soul must be greeted by such wonder. The cabin was still under construction the summer I turned sixteen. I came with my parents for a weekend. Uncle Lawrence, an architect, designed this A-frame cabin as a summer place. My mother and her younger sister, Aunt Lois, had plenty to talk about as the men hammered and nailed. The railing on the sleeping loft was not installed, and my parents slept in the one enclosed room upstairs. My bed was the couch downstairs, and I would wake as the sun sent slivers of light through the blinds. I feigned sleep as others came to life. Aunt Lois came out of her bedroom to make coffee. I listened to the bubbling and steaming noises of an electric percolator. When the first cup was poured, she carried it outside, walked down the stairs, and took the trail to the lake, fifty feet below. Her morning perch was on a lower deck, tucked under the trees, on the water. If she was in her bathing suit, I heard the splashes of her dive into the water, the strokes of her arms, the kicks of her feet. I rolled over and tried to return to sleep, but I knew I was missing out on something sacred. The wonder of a new day beginning.

    I don't want to miss a moment on this day, fifty-six years later. The morning sun will be on the deck only until eleven, and I delight in the tranquility and stillness, the opportunity to breathe deeply and listen with my heart to the earth's awakening. I have my journal and pen, and the coffee is ready. I look up at the meadow on Bead Lake Peak, 4,800 feet in height, a clearing accessible only on foot, where the ashes of my aunt and uncle have long been scattered. The cabin is mine now, in joint ownership with my sister. We have owned it since 1974. Less than a decade after he built it, Uncle Lawrence's Multiple Sclerosis affected his mobility and ability to climb stairs. They wanted the cabin to remain in the family, and we were happy to have the opportunity. Insurance money from my husband Bill's death in Viet Nam allowed me to buy in.

    The faded photo on the cabin wall reminds me how, on Labor Day, 1968, one month after our wedding, I brought my new husband to meet my favorite aunt and uncle and to share with him this beautiful place. Bill, taking in the view through his hazel eyes, dimples showing from his broad smile, was captivated. The camera always at hand, he took pictures, one which he later framed—two taken on the way up the Pend Oreille River, and one from this same deck, looking across the water at the meadow on Bead Lake Peak. We would return once more, four years later, with both our children, only six weeks before he died.

I feel his presence as I stand where the picture was taken. There are no branches in the picture. The trees have obviously grown another thirty feet in the last 52 years. The image on the wall shows how much the lake remains the same, and how much has changed. It reveals a time and place where we once sat on the deck, watching bats feeding on mosquitoes, gazing up at stars and satellites, and watching meteor showers. Now tree branches obscure the nighttime view.

What remains the same is the cabin. The fireplace, handcrafted of hand-selected boulders, is the focal point, reaching from beneath the foundation, through the center, extending into the vaulted ceiling—all stone and mortar, vented to heat both the main living space and the private bedroom on the other side. The loft has one walled-off bedroom, and the rest is open with a balcony, with overflow space for mattresses on the floor—an area for as many as ten warm bodies to play and to sleep. The steep metal roof allows heavy snow to slide off. Original tongue and groove cedar covers the walls and the ceiling. Hardwood, once waxed and polished annually, covers the floor; faded and tired linoleum tiles are in the kitchen and bathroom. The antique wood stove in the kitchen was once an additional heat source. It had been used by my aunt and my mother, women with firsthand knowledge from their childhood of how to stoke the fire and regulate the temperature for baking. It is now a convenient storage place for fresh fruit, loaves of bread, and other snacks, but the stovepipe is no longer in place.

What hasn't changed is the lake, three fingers spread out

into Kaniksu National forest, with only the lake's western side developed. There are four campsites scattered on the lake trail and a boat launch, used only by fishing boats, kayakers, and paddle-boarders. Given the appropriate name, "Bead" Lake, it resembles a necklace strung with three sparkling diamond pendants. The lake is 720 acres, the largest in Pend Oreille County, bordering Idaho, overshadowed by Priest Lake to the east and Lake Couer d'Alene to the South.

It is our wonder. A glacial creation with little wind, generally quiet and still, visited by ducks, geese, osprey, woodpeckers, and jays; squirrel, chipmunks, mice, deer, mink, raccoons, rabbits, and an occasional cougar.

Another photo of the lake is in my home office. Taken the same day by Bill, I am captured emerging from a swim. I grew up near freshwater lakes, took swim lessons every summer at the county swimming pool, loved water, and learned to water ski when I was twelve. It had been raining, but I dove in and exited the water quickly when the thunder and lightning began. I ran up the trail and breathlessly climbed the stairs as he asked me to stop and look up. My hands are raised to catch the rain, my hair slicked back from my swim, and the pearl pendant, his wedding present to me, glistens at my neck. One can see my love for this six ft. tall soldier, reflecting his infectious smile.

I yearn for more pictures of this time or even just one of him holding our second daughter. When he took leave from Viet Nam to meet our six-week-old baby girl, we came back to visit the cabin. In a time before phones became cameras with one in every pocket, Bill was behind the lens, recording moments. He captured images of me, constantly rocking a colicky baby girl and entertaining our three-year-old daughter. We expected many more years together to document our family life, but they never came. He was killed in action six weeks later.

Buying the cabin made sense in 1974 since it was a mere hour from Spokane, where I expected to live and raise my children in one place, near their grandparents. I wanted to stay home, raise my kids, and give them the stability I had of being nurtured and known in a single community for eighteen years. I yearned to replace the love of my life, a responsible, caregiving husband, with another just like him, believing I could not raise my children alone. Within eighteen months I married David, another six-foot tall soldier, with freckles in place of dimples and red hair instead of brown. He made me laugh again and entertained my children. Our first date had been on his ski boat on another freshwater lake nearby, swimming in the moonlight. He had been discharged from the service after his tour in Viet Nam. I believed we would never have to talk about the war, and we never did. We ignored his psychic wounds as well as my deep grief and disillusionment. I endured the silence and secrets between us for seven years.

Not working outside the home, I had the luxury of spending most of every summer at the cabin. The daughter we had together was parked in her playpen on the deck from the time she was nine months old, and like my own childhood, each of my three girls took to the water like fish—diving, swimming, and spending hours floating on air mattresses and inner tubes. I swam with them, resumed water skiing, and advanced to my slalom ski.

We did our best to live by the rules Aunt Lois, a kindergarten teacher, had in place.

1. Bring everything you might need with you.

2. Once you come to the cabin, there is no reason to drive the eight miles to the nearest town for ANYTHING.

3. Take a walk on the trail into the forest every day.

4. If you see wildflowers, you must count ten of them before you pick one.

5. Sweep the stairs and the floors and change the sheets before you leave.

In our appearance-driven married life, David and I bundled up for a winter weekend with the church youth group, kept the fire blazing, and watched teenagers slide across the frozen lake. We hosted my siblings and their families over Fourth of July weekends, with hours of water skiing, an abundance of food, and fireworks reflected in the water. We shared our paradise with friends. During those visits, David entertained with tales of his plans for real estate developments, buying property at low prices, improving it, and selling for a profit. He persuaded friends and relatives to invest their savings. He was deceptive and dishonest when things went wrong. Before David filed for bankruptcy, he showed up one weekend with his head bandaged and his arm in a sling after a day of boating and drinking. My illusion of security vanished. He said he never liked my oldest daughter since she declared at four, "YOU are not MY Daddy." I began spending weeks at the cabin, hours sailing on a lake with no wind, walking the trails, crying where no one could see me, and seeking life choices for a future for my kids.

Two years of indecision later, my second marriage ended, the ski boat was gone, and I was back in college, preparing for a profession to provide for my family. I shared my frustration and fears with the pastor of my church. Larry was also single, parenting two kids after his wife declared she no longer wanted to be a pastor's wife or a mother. He listened well to me, understood my laments, and helped me find a way forward, affirming my educational goals and encouraging my interest in sociology, and my excitement about theology. The possibility of becoming a pastor, utilizing my life experiences of grief and loss, inspired me.

Larry was physically different in every way. Overweight and short enough that I didn't have to crane my neck upwards for a kiss. He was attentive to me and supportive of my dreams. He, too had been an Army officer stationed in Germany during the Vietnam years. This third marriage added two step-children to my family. We moved across the state so I could attend seminary. This was the first of six relocations, each a six or seven hours drive from the lake

Our visits to the cabin became a sacred, dedicated, ritual time. We always took our two-week vacation there, first with all five kids, scheduled around the dates of Church Camp, thirty miles from the cabin. One week, my middle daughter would go to church camp; the next week, my oldest. When we were all together, games of Hearts, Oh Hell, and Rummy kept us up late into the night. S'mores completed every meal, whether over the dying briquets on the barbeque grill or in the embers in the fireplace. Lightning storms were best at night; our private light show from our picture windows. Rainy days kept us in front of the fire, bent over Jigsaw puzzles that overtook the dining table. Endless games of Uno, competitive Scrabble tournaments, and side-by-side Solitare with actual cards instead of computer screens filled those days. There was no TV, no internet connection, and no cell phones.

As our kids grew independent, they invited their own set of friends. They wanted the time to follow their own macrobiotic, organic diets or engage in recreational drugs without our supervision. Soon Larry and I were coming alone, each with a dozen books saved up throughout the year for just this time. Historical novels for Larry, detective novels, and books by women authors for me. During the five years it took to complete my dissertation, I hauled boxes of theological research back and forth but seldom touched the work. Larry was not one to enjoy outdoor activities, was overweight, short of breath, and prone to falling if he walked the trails. He did not know how to swim. I frequently invited a girlfriend or a work colleague, sometimes my sister from Texas; or anyone to come to play with me to attend local outdoor arts and crafts fairs. Fabric and patterns and my sewing machine replaced puzzles on cold, rainy, solitary days.

When our children's marriages and babies came, the beds filled again, and laughter replaced the silence of a tired, middle-aged, mid-life crisis-surviving, long-married couple. Hours of water time, large noisy suppers, and late-night games filled the spaces between us. After Larry's kidney failure and his needs turned to keeping a sterilized environment for dialysis and requisite quiet for daily naps. Then each family became more comfortable choosing a different weekend. Larry and I came alone.

Moving equipment, ordering supplies, and making emergency trips to the nearest hospital fell on me. Packing food for two weeks, loading and unloading the car, cooking, cleaning, and washing dishes every day, made cabin time less vacation than giving full-time care to someone with complications. Again, the lake calmed me as I used my kayak to provide silence and space for myself, savoring the luxury of solitude. I was on the water more than I was in it. Swimming and then hauling myself out of the water onto the dock became difficult. The echoes of children's laughter were missing. The rules of cabin life have long since been rewritten.

That was our routine for Larry's final three years. I returned to the cabin for a week two weeks after he died. I came with children, grandchildren, and a box of ashes, which I set on top of the dresser in our bedroom, where it rested for two summers.

This day, the morning of my seventy-second birthday, the sky is filled with pure light. I am warmed by the sun. My mother's afghan has slipped from my shoulders. My reverie ends. I return to the bedroom and retrieve the box of ashes. I scatter them over the edge of the deck, leaving small traces of the one who was never fully engaged as father or stepfather, seldom comfortable in our boisterous family. "Larry is not here—he will always be here." All the family will come to visit without interaction, much like it was when he was alive. I reach for my journal and write—

In this place, I am every age between sixteen and seventy-two. Every memory converges here—every laugh and every tear—every desire and every regret. This is my home place, the center of my spirit, the keeper of my story, the bearer of my pain, and my legacy to my children, grandchildren, and their children. I have little else to leave to them. They require nothing more.

DYING WELL

"RED. RED! RED!!"

I heard my husband's voice, calm and gentle, with an unfamiliar urgency. I was explaining my testiness of the day and telling him about the reason for last night's insomnia. I also happened to be driving, waving my right hand to make my point.

Irritated by his interruption, I glanced at him to ensure he was listening. I noticed a look of concern on his face, then turned my eyes back to the intersection, realizing the traffic light was indeed RED, as the car coming towards us slammed on its brakes instead of making the turn. One way or another, there could have been a T-bone crash. If I had been in the passenger's seat, I would have gasped loudly, pressed my right foot on my imaginary brake, reached out to grab his arm, and raised my voice to shout, "Stop! Didn't you see that red light?" My shallow breathing and heart palpitations would have continued until he would sigh, and remind me that he was the one who had never been involved in an accident.

I kept moving through the intersection, surprised by the slowness of my reflexes. I approached the next light as the adrenaline kicked in.

"You must have a lot on your mind," my husband gently said.

"Why, yes, I do," came out in a quiver. "But right now, I almost got us killed. Maybe I need to stop driving— give up my car. My mother made that decision when she blew through a stop sign. Thankfully, no one was hurt. But she was eighty...."

I had been fretting about the potential for chaos following the 2020 election. In our isolation due to the COVID-19 pandemic, I felt there was little I could control or influence.

There was only so much stress I could handle. I avoided newscasts and political commentary but had watched a small portion of the vice-presidential debate the night before. My thoughts kept me awake half the night. I wanted to share my concerns, air my fears, vent my frustrations, and feel heard, dissipating my anxiety as I did so. Running a red light was only a symptom of my distraction.

As they often do, my thoughts drifted to the question of how I might die. Driving into Montana two months earlier, I noticed white roadside crosses. Sometimes one solitary cross, sometimes groups of two, three, or more. I was the navigator on our Motor Home journey to National Parks, and the legend on the map I held in my lap explained, "White markers show fatalities and serve as a reminder to drive safely, drive sober, and wear seatbelts."

The crosses began my annual review of those I have loved who died during the summer months. I mentally checked off names and dates— two husbands, my father, my mother, my sister, one niece, and last summer, my brother Bill who died on my birthday, July 25, 2019. Of course, there is death in other seasons—each life-changing, heartbreaking, earth-shaking.

It is not death that worries me. I am content in my understanding that death may well be the end of my physical existence, and I trust in the idea of God, who will sort out what may or may not be next. I spent twenty-seven years of my life in professional ministry, helping others celebrate the well-lived lives of their loved ones. I relied on my own experiences of grief and loss to be available to listen, to receive others' suffering, to let their questions sit safely between us, and to offer solace in memorializing stories of fidelity and unconditional love. I am at peace with the inevitable fact of being dead. It is the manner of dying that fills my thoughts.

The unfortunate coincidence of election years magnifies my concern. I was widowed by the war in Vietnam in 1972 due to decisions made a world away from my innocent childhood farm life. I became fatherless in 1976 when my dad died of bone marrow cancer, most likely caused by working downwind from radioactive materials released from the Hanford Nuclear Reservation near Richland, Washington, during another time of world conflict. Life is affected by who is in charge. World leaders, elections, and everyday decisions have consequences. Each cause of death is circumstantial, unavoidable, and unexplainable.

Twenty years ago – while the world was reeling from planes crashing into the World Trade Center in New York, the Pentagon in Washington D.C., and the heroic sacrifice of passengers on a plane in Pennsylvania – my world collapsed more privately. A weekend of unexplained abdominal pain sent me to my primary care doctor, who sent me to an emergency room for a CT scan. As I was wheeled away from the machine and into the hallway, I asked the technician if there was anything to worry about. His cryptic response was, "We found a mass on your kidney. But you have two of them. It's a good thing it's not on your liver."

The journey to diagnosis was brief. Within a week I saw a nephrologist, who showed me images of a growth half again the size of my left kidney. The doctor declared I had cancer. There was not much more I heard at that point. He continued to my choice of treatment options—letting it go (and grow) and checking on it every six months, or removing it. I asked about the surgery option, how much recovery time, when I could return to work, and how soon surgery could be scheduled. I felt the urgency to ask only one question before I left his office, "But, why are you saying I have cancer?"

"Because that's what it is."

My mother, my father, three aunts, half a dozen cousins, and countless parishioners who all died of cancer were on my mind when I declared I did not want to be burned by radiation or poisoned by chemotherapy. "Just cut it out," I demanded.

On Halloween 2001, they did just that. The six weeks I gave myself for recovery helped me learn how to ask for help when I needed it, relying on others for meals and assistance with showers. I continued to tire quickly through December and came to understand the term "major surgery completely." My determination to "not die" was a factor in my recovery, but the call from my surgeon saying, "it was just a tumor," that there were no malignant cells and no need for follow-up treatments, made the most significant difference. I refer to it as my "small-c cancer," but it hasn't stopped my worry about dying.

I was an expert in dodging when others turned to me for answers to their faith questions about death and, more particularly, the ultimate questions of heaven and hell. After Bill, my brother died, I was asked by one of his sisters-in-law if I had asked him whether he had "accepted Jesus-Christ-as-his-Lord-and-Savior." I had visited him the week before his final surgery for lung cancer, certain it would be my last opportunity to see him. His diminished verbal abilities hampered our conversation due to a series of small strokes and the memory losses of an eighty-year-old.

It was clear Bill had been engaged in life review, telling me that he regretted never really getting to know me. A decade my senior, he joined the Navy when I was eight years old. He returned to the family farm when our father died, and for the last thirty-five years, we lived three hundred miles apart, coming together only for family funerals—our mother, sister, aunts, and uncles. Still, and always, he called me his "baby sister."

I presided at his Memorial service. I reviewed his faithfulness in his marriage of forty-nine years, his pride in his six grandsons and one granddaughter, his work ethic and contribution to the life of his community, his patriotism, and his love of country. I could honestly declare his legacy an example of a life well lived. My answer to his sister-in-law was that the question never came up. I trusted in God to sort out Bill's place in heaven.

I never tried to extract such a confession from a parishioner, but if asked the same question by a family member, I would not lie. I could constantly reassure them that the person I knew had a place in God's heart, had lived life well, and was forgiven. I seldom thought about the source of the question, nor understood how deeply ingrained the concern for eternal life remains.

Disease, violence, and political instability have influenced world views and changed theology and church policies. In times of plague and earlier pandemics, awareness of the fragility of life caused the shift from concern over humanity's collective judgment at the end of time (fueled by apocalyptic biblical imagery) to questions of individual judgment immediately after death (concern about personal salvation). One's own death and judgment were often seen as issues that required preparation. While training for parish work, Priests were expected to minister to the dying. In the 15th century, The Ars Moriendi, or "The Art of Dying, Well," was written; a treatise with six chapters that prescribed rites and prayers to be used at the time of death. A second book illustrated the dying person's struggle with temptations before attaining a good death. These were practical manuals to inform the dying about what to expect and guided their actions and attitudes that would lead to confession of sins, repentance, a "good death," and salvation.

These teachings survived for centuries and were revised and rewritten by Anglican, Lutheran, and other Protestant expressions of Christianity. The ritualization of the pain and grief of dying became manageable and conventional through Christian belief, prayer, and practice.

My vocation of pastoral ministry was at times influenced by historical practices of the Christian faith, sometimes surprised by ingrained fears of hell and damnation. The techniques of medical care in these days of a new pandemic isolate and marginalize the dying. The work of Hospice and palliative care provide a different framework, with the dying person at the center of attention. It was in that work that I found a purpose, to remind others that living well is essential for a good death.

The one who gave me life taught me the most about living. From my mother, I learned to love without reservation, give without stinginess, forgive wrongs easily, listen deeply, embrace hope, trust completely, laugh openly, and know how to die.

Growing up, I knew the kitchen as the heartbeat of our home. The kitchen door was never locked, and everyone entered and exited through that center on the farm. Family, community, and church filled our lives, but no matter the events of her day, Mother managed a meal on the table, and we sat down to eat together.

In summer, the annual grain harvest meant four full meals a day for a crew of six: breakfast at 7:00, dinner at noon, sandwich lunch in the field at 3:30 pm, and supper at 7 pm. All came off with precision, Monday through Saturday, for two to three weeks, determined by rain delays or interruptions caused by mechanical breakdowns. Mother and daughters worked fourteen-hour shifts in the kitchen, the men twelve-hour shifts in the fields.

A hearty breakfast was the meal Mother managed on her own. I would wake to the lingering smells of bacon and the aroma of coffee, with my first job a sink full of dishes. Syrup residue from plates of buttermilk pancakes, the bacon drippings, and particles of fried eggs and hash browns were scrapped off and washed away. By the time everything was rinsed and dried by hand, dinner, the noon meal, was in earnest production.

With precision, and recipes committed to memory, yeast was dissolved in warm water, milk, eggs, sugar, and butter added, flour mixed in and kneaded by hand, given an hour to rise and double in size, punched down, rolled out to be spread with butter, sprinkled with generous quantities of sugar and cinnamon, rolled up, sliced, laid in a pan of melted butter, and topped with a mixture of brown sugar and milk, two dozen sweet rolls were set aside to raise another hour. The rhythm was hypnotic. Peas shelled, beans snapped, or corn shucked; apples or peaches peeled and sliced, while my Mother mixed flour, lard, and salt, sprinkled it with water, blended it, patted it into a ball, and rolled out pie crusts, measured out sugar, flour, cinnamon, and nutmeg, stirred the fruit together, filled two pie pans, decorated the top crust, sealed the edges, brushed the tops with milk and sugar, and set them in the oven.

At the right time, meat was set on to roast or fry, potatoes boiled or baked, lettuce washed and tossed, rolls replaced pies in the oven, and at the first sound of a truck on the gravel, the frantic dance of serving began. Basins of hot water were carried out to the yard, set on the picnic bench, with bars of gray Lava soap beside them. Boiling water would be poured over eight tea bags in the teapot. The tea had time to steep while the men washed up, then it was poured into a gallon jar filled with ice. The crew took their places at the table, serving dishes were passed, their glasses were filled with tea, and sweet rolls disappeared. We offered seconds and thirds, and then the women could eat before we washed dishes and started over again.

Widowed at the age of sixty-one, Mother left the farming community where she was born. Marrying a lifetime friend, my mother and stepfather had fourteen years to enjoy the adventures of world travel, and frequent visits with kids and grandkids. They lived in cooperative housing with two of her sisters, each having their own apartment. A brother-in-law had built the complex in the middle of a forty-acre orchard overlooking the city of Spokane. It was designed as a retirement center for the family. There were six private units, a great common room with an indoor swimming pool, and a gathering space for family reunions.

When widowed again at the age of seventy-six, Mother visited more frequently, and we had hours for her to share the stories of her life. I became her confidante, celebrated the pioneer heritage of my grandparents, and learned from her tales of sacrifice and survival. She admitted that her second marriage had delayed her grief over my father's death, and she freely shared details of their life together, wanting someone to know the stories that had been theirs alone. I took comfort in her confession, "We weren't always perfectly suited for each other, but we had a good life!"

Her eightieth birthday was the milestone that allowed us to celebrate her resilience and independence. In late August, we hosted an open house inviting friends from the first sixty years of her life on the farm and included family members from around the country. Nieces and nephews and family groups with step-children, grandchildren, and great-grandchildren posed for pictures with the birthday girl. The obligatory picture with her six surviving sisters shows them lined up beside the poster highlighting her world travels in her eightieth year.

After the guests left, she announced her decision to give up her car and move into a retirement home.

It would be over a year before Mother located just the right place. It was March when she, my Aunt Rhoda, and Uncle Herbert moved into Park Place, Senior Housing. In her new three-room apartment, there was only space for a single bed and her dresser, a dinette set with two chairs, her hide-a-bed, rocking chair, TV, and sewing machine. She left spices and bakers' tools behind: stationery boxes of personal correspondence: collections labeled "cards too nice to throw away," and a shelf of personal journals. I rented a U-Haul to take more significant pieces of furniture 300 miles to my home.

It was easy to suspect that the moving process had worn her out, but her body began to tell her there was something more. On the Monday after Easter, surgery to remove her gall bladder revealed a tumor, and the tumor was diagnosed as pancreatic cancer. Three months to a year, they told me. Three good months, and then who knows...?

I began to make week-long visits, beginning with her hospitalization and helping her settle back into her apartment. I came for doctor appointments, providing a second set of ears, hearing facts, and discerning the truth for myself. I clearly remember Dr. Escandon telling us there was no way to remove or slow the growth of her cancer. Mother was equally clear, informing him that she did not want to suffer as my father had from the multiple myeloma that ate away the marrow in his spine. Dr. Escandon assured her there had been advances in medicine in the last twenty years and promised he would keep her pain-free.

We were in her apartment three days after surgery, watching "Jeopardy" and "Wheel of Fortune." She was aware of the possibilities and the ultimate reality. She was patient and stoic, and wise, demonstrating great courage and dignity. Silenced by her determination and composure, I listened as she told me these things:

She would not tell anyone that what she had was incurable.

She has no one to forgive or seek forgiveness from.

She is afraid to die alone.

I silently vowed to honor her wishes, to support her decisions.

I spent the remainder of the week sorting and packing what remained in her previous apartment. I spent a day deciding what I might keep or give to my daughters, and how to dispose of a lifetime collection of a baker's tools. The task was overwhelming, the memories of her life in everything I touched. I planned to return in time to eat with her, thinking we would find our place in the dining room for another bland, unsalted institutional meal. She called several times, asking when I would be back. I heard the loneliness in her voice and decided to let some of the packing go.

I arrived at the Senior Center. The table was set. A nephew had brought a freshly caught trout when he visited. Green beans, a green salad with mandarin oranges and homemade dressing, potatoes, and freshly made sweet rolls accompanied the fried trout, with an apple pie for dessert. The thinness of her face, the slump of her shoulders, made it clear: what was once effortless had taken everything out of her. She was still who she had been all her life—the one who gave without counting the cost.

As I prepared to leave, Mother announced that she had decided to resume her quilting, nap less, and enjoy as much of each day as she could.

The hide-a-bed was in constant use; the sewing machine kept

humming as I encouraged her to make more blocks for the final quilt for the youngest of fifteen granddaughters. I wanted to keep her engaged in this world a little longer. I encouraged old friends to come for a visit, sooner rather than later. When they arrived, they knew, without words, that they were saying goodbye.

Between my trips, my sister Sue came from Ohio for a week. Mary Ann, a step-daughter-in-law who was also a nurse, came from New York and stayed with her for another. Mary Ann shared her medical expertise with me and gave some advice on caregiving. I knew it was time to be there. I needed to be with her, to stay through to the end. I arrived on Sunday, and shortly after I arrived, Mother expressed her concern that I needed to eat. It was the last coherent, "like her" remark she made until the following day.

I woke to discover that Mom had not made it to the bathroom during the night. After changing her nightgown, I suggested breakfast. Anything she wanted. She shook her head. I went for the Ensure, poured it into a glass, and lifted it to her mouth. She kept her lips closed tight. She would not drink. Through my tears, I pleaded, "Mother, you can't just stop eating." She lifted her eyes, looked into mine, and said her final words, "Yes, I can."

By that afternoon, a hospital bed had been delivered. The kitchen was the only place the bed could go. I moved the dinette set into a corner. A nurse came and inserted a catheter. Dr. Escandon made a house call, and said to her, "You don't have much time left." It was as if she decided that was okay, good enough for her.

My mother slept. Trays of food were delivered on schedule from the dining room. Except for nibbles I managed to swallow, they were returned down the hall, out of sight, to the central kitchen, untouched. My birthday came, and Aunt Rhoda insisted I leave for lunch. She would stay with Mother, reading to her. I sat through a green light until horns began honking behind me, lost in thought, trying to imagine losing my mother on my forty-eighth birthday.

For three nights, I fitfully listened from the bedroom to the slow, rattling breath of the one who had given me life and inspired my own living. My daughters arrived and set up the hide-a-bed. Throughout the day, we held vigil. We made sure she heard our voices. We were sitting beside her in the kitchen, talking to her and telling stories. Laughing. Crying some. Loving her with our presence to the end.

She died on her own terms, without invasive surgery, unnecessary Chemotherapy or radiation, and attendant nausea and hair loss. She had time to say all that needed to be said, to celebrate the goodness of life, then lay it down without regrets. There was something majestic about her body's ability to shut itself down. We watched her chest rise and fall one last time.

My mother taught me to die well. Not the part about keeping the seriousness of her pancreatic cancer a secret, but the part about inviting loved ones to come for a visit sooner rather than later. 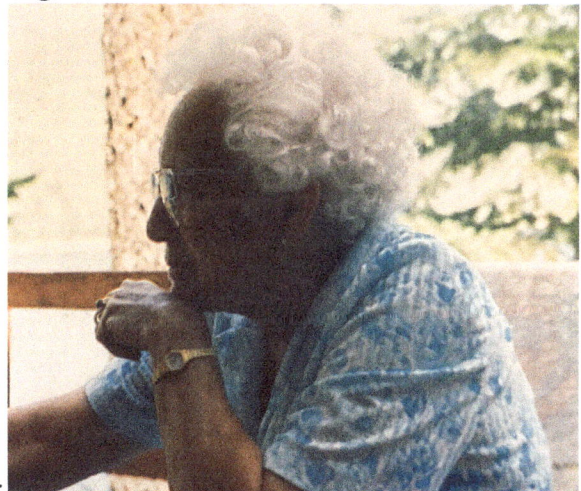 Together we learned from her courage; we bask in her attitude without worry; we celebrate living each day.

Dorothy Green Monk Jacobson
September 18, 1914 —July 28, 1996

JEAN GANT DELASTRADA

Stories Of Differences

OUTLIERS

THE SECRETARY AT MY OFFICE KEEPS A BOWL OF M&M'S on her counter for all who come by. I find myself scanning the dish for the misshapen candies, my first choice. If there are none, I calculate what color there are the least of, and take them.

I prefer the heels of the bread, the rice stuck to the bottom of the pan. I eat the broken crackers in the box first. I am seldom interested in pie until there is only one small, stale piece left. I pass when the cake is cut and served, but feel compelled to eat the crumbs of cake and lines of frosting left on the plate.

In high school, I was voted runner-up to "Most Likely to Succeed." I felt exposed as if my classmates were taunting me, and somehow knew I would be a failure. When I scored 162 on my fifth-grade IQ test and was told I was smarter than 99% of the people in the world, I didn't know enough to question what, if anything, this really meant. I was terrified. There was so much I didn't understand—if all these other people around me understood even less, we were in trouble!

I was a Yankee growing up in the South. My father, back in New Jersey, was crazy, so I couldn't see him or talk about him, couldn't be anything like him. Who was I? I wasn't even a real girl—I was fascinated by frogs and lizards, and couldn't pretend to be afraid of spiders and snakes. I grew up to marry the black sheep of a large Catholic family. When I became a teacher, my favorite students were the sensitive, intelligent ones, especially those at the painful extremes of difference.

I became a special education teacher and taught emotionally-disturbed children. In the mid-nineties, a boy I worked with was given the new diagnosis of Asperger's Syndrome. I was his case manager, working with him at home on learning to live with his family (and them with him). At eleven, CJ was gifted in math and science, but couldn't tolerate the uncertainties of loading the dishwasher. If he didn't have the right number of plates and cups to fill it exactly, he would scream and throw the dishes.

I helped CJ clean his room, in his own fashion, and he showed me his collections of plastic bread fasteners and dried glue he had pulled from his fingertips. As a reward for doing his chores, CJ asked me to take him to the library to read the Revised Code of Washington. I learned to explain the social world to him in terms he could understand, and he responded with his ultimate compliment, "You couldn't be a human from this planet!"

I was fascinated with CJ, his abilities, and his quirks, and surprised at how easily I could understand and communicate with him. Being with him was strangely familiar, in an exciting way. I learned everything I could about Asperger's and autism and began to look at the people in my personal life and history in a new light.

DOWNLOADING SUCCESS

IN 2005, I CELEBRATED a first in my career—the college graduation of a former client. I had been CJ's case manager for ten years. Despite his diagnosis of Asperger's Syndrome, he had won a national contest in computer hardware repair in high school and received a scholarship to a technical college. CJ maintained a 4.0 average in his college classes, without any ADA accommodations. He was the star of his school and family, and silly with pride and excitement. This was my success story as well as his.

Several months later, I heard that CJ had begun a full-time job designing parts for airplane seats, and was in love with a girl at work. A year later, I called for the latest updates on his successes. But things weren't going so well for CJ anymore.

As he himself summarized his downfall, "I had a crush on a coworker, couldn't concentrate on my work, and got laid off. Now I'm afraid if I get another job the same thing will happen again." I winced at this all too typical example of the difficulties of living with autism.

I started working with CJ when he was eleven years old. He was fascinated with Pascal's Theorem and his favorite reading was the Revised Code of Washington. But he would scream at his little sister Donna and call her names if she mispronounced a word, and couldn't tolerate sitting within six feet of another student at school. As his case manager, I spent half a day a week in his world, supporting his efforts to connect with the outside social world.

For several years I spent most Saturday afternoons with CJ at his house, helping him get along with his family and do chores.

I came to dread the rainy afternoons when CJ's mother Karen greeted me with, "CJ and Doug had a big fight and trashed their room again!"

Here's what would usually come next::

I started calmly, brightly, hoping to shift the tone of crisis, "OK, are you ready to work together to clean it up?"

"I can't! It's too much! Anyway, CJ did it!" Doug cried, reaching his arms out to his mother to save him.

"Whiny little brat!" CJ responded. "He poured out his toy box on my bed, so I threw it all on the floor. Then he tried to break my lego models, so I pushed him into the shelf and it fell down."

CJ, at twelve, was only three years older than his brother but seemed twice his size. Both boys were handsome, healthy-looking, blue-eyed blondes, but CJ was more sturdily built, His face was largely expressionless, slightly smug, and mean-looking when he was angry. In contrast, Doug was slim and wiry, throwing his whole body around with dramatic emotion.

I could hardly see the floor of the bedroom for the mix of toys, dirty clothes, and blankets. CJ sat on his bed, rebuilding a lego ship, while Doug held onto his mother in the doorway.

"Let's take turns cleaning up, and then I'll take both of you out for a treat, OK?" I offered.

"OK, help me find the rest of my legos that BABY spilled on the floor!" CJ directed me, while Doug and his mother went into the kitchen to fix lunch. It was a long, slow process, but no more fighting and the boys even agreed on where to go for a treat!

The bedroom-trashing fights continued week after week, and it became clear that my interventions weren't changing things for Karen and the boys. Karen and I gave up. CJ had been withdrawing to the old trailer next to the house to play alone, and when he turned thirteen Karen said,

"CJ, what would you think of keeping all your things in

the trailer, and just sleeping in the bedroom with Doug?"

"Far out!" CJ said, "Can you help me move, Jean?"

"Can't he sleep out there, too?" Doug asked hopefully.

"It's not fair!" came the usual screech from Donna, but she had her own room, and no one paid her much attention.

CJ and I packed up his toys, books, and collections in cardboard boxes and took them out to the trailer. He spread his sleeping bag on the built-in platform at one end of the trailer and used milk crates and boards to build shelves at the other end. Now my Saturday visits were busy with taking things out of the boxes and putting them on the shelves.

The boxes were never completely unpacked, of course. CJ would take out one thing and admire it or talk about it, then look for the best spot for it on his shelves. And his collections grew—film cans filled with pencil shavings, dried glue, and miscellaneous hardware. He collected traffic reflectors and "road turtles", the bright yellow lumps of concrete used as highway markers. He made a chain from plastic bread bag fasteners and strung it from wall to wall. One sunny day he pointed out to me how the light illuminated dust particles in the air inside the trailer, and we moved around to see it change from different angles.

I loved these times of being in CJ's world, sharing his delight with simple physical things. It was a refreshing change from the hours of urging him to do chores and take turns with his brother and sister. I think it was because I spent time in his world that CJ became willing to spend time in the complicated, unpredictable social world with me.

When I took CJ to a birthday party for a neighbor boy, he kept asking me, "What do I do next?" I took him to Boy Scout meetings, where he was more interested in arranging the chalk in the chalkboard tray than talking and playing with the other boys. One evening he spent an hour studying a book about knot-making, then went home and made lego models of the different types of knots.

Meanwhile, at school CJ was bounced back and forth between highly capable classes and behavior disorder classes. He seldom hurt others physically, but adults and children alike were afraid of his verbal threats and insults, his screams of rage when things didn't go his way, and his moving around the classroom and school building at will. Once when I visited his middle school classroom, he went to get a drink of water from the cooler, couldn't find a cup, and screamed at his teacher, "Do you expect me to pick up the jug of water and pour it over my head?" As the teacher started to call Security, I prompted him, "Wait, CJ. Say, 'I need a cup.'"

CJ's brother and the other younger neighborhood boys looked up to him with awe and fear, and wanted his ideas and help with making forts and fighting wars in the wooded vacant lot across the street. CJ wanted to play, and enjoyed his "top dog" status, but had a short fuse for the younger boys 'limitations. Most of their games disintegrated with CJ yelling, "No, not that way! I can destroy that fort with one kick! Idiot!"

When CJ decided to build a private fort, I talked him through his frustrations with the vagaries of hammers and nails. He collected scrap lumber, measured the pieces, and drew diagrams, then raged when he couldn't get the corners to square perfectly. I held boards in place, gave advice about approximation (all of which he rejected), and moved out of the way when he threw the hammer. My strongest skill at times like this was an understatement, and being sure my voice went down at the end of sentences. "Let's take a break and go to 7-11 for a Slurpee," I'd say casually.

Getting a Slurpee every week was the routine that grounded our relationship for ten years. Once I made the mistake of saying, "If you can't finish loading the dishwasher in ten minutes, we won't have time for a Slurpee." CJ turned on me, screaming, "I thought you knew that kind of pressure doesn't work for me!"

I learned to avoid the explicit, "first/then" and found unique activities to do after CJ did his chores. We would take long drives on the county roads, looking for road turtles that had come unglued, and I'd pull off the street while CJ, watching carefully for traffic, ran out to the middle of the road to pick them up. I would take him to the hardware store to look at magnets and ropes and extension cords. The boy who couldn't have other children anywhere near him would get into long conversations with the older hardware store clerks about electricity, magnetism, and the tensile strength of ropes.

These things CJ understood. I searched for ways to help him understand the unpredictable ways of people. His younger brother Doug adored CJ and put up with his ordering him around the house, but abandoned his weird brother when the neighbor boys invited him to go ride bikes. His sister Donna squealed and shrieked any time CJ poked her or pulled her hair. He couldn't resist the thrill of provoking this reaction, then was offended when their mother yelled at him to stop.

Week after week, I tried to interpret to CJ the feelings and reactions of those around him. I taught him to withdraw to his trailer when his frustration at his family's human foibles exploded. We talked at length about his dream of living alone in a cabin in the woods when he turned eighteen. CJ came to appreciate the interactions of the family dogs and cats. "They're not manipulative." When he said to me, "You couldn't be a human from this planet!" I asked, "Is that a compliment?" "Of course," he answered.

In the late nineties, teenaged CJ discovered computers, and with them new ways of relating to other people. At home, he fought with his brother and sister so relentlessly for computer time that his mother helped him scrounge enough computer parts from Goodwill for him to assemble his own computer. CJ had been sleeping in the trailer to avoid the constant bickering that occurred when he shared the small bedroom with his brother. He persuaded his mother to let him set up his computer in the trailer and created a world of his own there.

CJ strung wires out from the house for electricity and internet connections, and only left the trailer to eat, shower, and go to school. When I came to help him do chores and errands, CJ invited me into the trailer, told me about the friends he'd met in chat rooms, and offered to show me his favorite porn site. When I under-reacted with, "CJ, I'm your counselor, you can't show me that," he got angry and accused me of not being his friend. The internet became his second, and more important, world. When his mother's boyfriend Jack disconnected his internet to discipline him, CJ fought back explosively, "You can't take away my internet rights!"

In high school, CJ's internet knowledge started to give him more status with his classmates. He, in turn, became more social. He also, apparently, became more interested in impressing his peers. One school day morning I got a panicked call from his mother Karen..

"The school just called. CJ's been boasting to the other kids that he knows how to make dynamite. He said he got the recipe over the internet."

"So are they worried that he's really going to do it?" I asked. "CJ likes to talk about blowing things up, but I think he's too safety-conscious to really do it."

"They thought it might be some kind of a prank, that he might try it to get attention." This was before 911 and the age of terrorism, fortunately.

"They just want to send CJ home for the day, for us to go through his trailer with him and be sure he doesn't have the ingredients. But you know how he is about his privacy. Can you come explain, so he won't freak out while Jack and I go through his things?"

CJ was pacing in front of the trailer door when I got there. "I told them I **knew how** to make dynamite. I never said I was gonna **do** it! Why don't they believe me?"

"They just want to be sure, because it's dangerous. You're not in trouble." My reassurances felt lame, even to me.

"Don't close the door! Don't touch anything!" CJ yelled in protest when Karen and Jack went into his trailer. He hovered by the trailer door, looking in anxiously, angrily wiping his tears away.

I tried to distract him with talk, "I wonder if your friends told on you because they were scared?"

"They're **not** my friends," CJ yelled. "I hate that school and everybody in it! I should have really blown it up!"

Karen and Jack bent over to climb out of the trailer. Jack carried a small box of matches, "We'd better keep these in the kitchen. You've got too much junk in that trailer to light matches. It's a firetrap!"

Karen moved in front of Jack before CJ could lunge at him, "It's OK, honey. We're done. I'll call the school, and you can stay home today, and go back tomorrow."

CJ pushed past us into his trailer and slammed the door shut. "Leave me alone!" he screamed and began to sob loudly.

We left him to regain his dignity, and the school took him back without further consequences.

We all thought he had learned, but people with autism have a hard time generalizing. Next, he hacked into the school district's administrative website. The technology department complained that they would have to hire an outside specialist to repair the damage, but his career counselor said, "Wait—CJ did it, I bet he can fix it." CJ not only repaired the firewall, he became a computer tutor for other students and a troubleshooter for the school's computers.

At home, CJ filled his trailer with broken computer

components to work on. Family life and social events continued to be challenging, but CJ found his niche in talking about computers. While his brother mowed lawns and his sister babysat, CJ found odd jobs repairing the home computers of neighbors and family friends

CJ took all the classes at the school's computer center, and the computer teacher guided him through local, state, and national computer competitions. At national his second year, CJ won his gold ribbon in computer hardware repair, and his college scholarship.

College brought more independence and consistent success. CJ's school time was dominated by electronics and computer studies; he was in his element. He rode his bike three miles to and from classes each day, then learned to drive and got a driver's license. He studied with fellow students and even socialized with them between classes. CJ seemed to be proving the notion that people with Asperger's can develop social skills on their own timeline, around their special interests.

Indeed, the setback CJ suffered when he fell in love would fit right in with the theory that social skills for people with Asperger's develop at two-thirds the rate of the typically developing. CJ at twenty-one responded to the prospect of a girlfriend as a fourteen-year-old might. This, at least, is what I told myself to temper my disappointment at the bad news. I hoped that he would have the support, and luck, to be a successful adult by thirty-five!

BAD GENES AND ROBOTS

"**WELL, HERE WE ARE.** Let's have a cup of tea." Mori sighed and settled herself on her futon. Finally, we could get back to our comfortable ritual!

I had just flown in from Seattle late the night before, but Mori insisted she was ready to come home from the hospital this morning. She was bouncing back from gall bladder surgery remarkably well for an eighty-five-year-old who was still recovering from last year's broken hip.

"Once the hospital workers' strike was over and they did the surgery, I was fine," Mori began her story. "But after five days on morphine waiting for surgery, I didn't know where I was. I was sure the doctor said my heart had stopped and they were going to send it in a box down the East River. Then they gave me Haldol, and ever since there are holes in my thinking. I remembered when Paul was on Haldol and he just wasn't himself, even though it stopped the delusions. Then I realized I need to tell you about Paul, while I still can. Come sit here." She patted the cushion next to her.

I brought our teacups over from the kitchen area of the small apartment, and sat at the other end of the futon, turning to face Mori. Her body was more twisted and frail than ever, but her eyes were lucid and her voice commanding. Whenever I visited my stepmother, our reminiscences over tea were our best way to share all the years I had missed, not knowing her, my father, and my half-brother Paul. I was thirsty for every detail, and she was eager to share minute, detailed memories with her only surviving family member.

"You know I told you that Paul left his jazz studies in the City when he was 20, and moved to Boston, then moved back home? Well, it was because he had a breakdown. We finally got him to a psychiatrist, and it was paranoid schizophrenia. He was in a mental hospital for a while, and that's when they put him on the Haldol."

"So—is that what he died of?" I asked, trying to reconfigure the pieces of the stories she'd told me about Paul.

"No, it wasn't the schizophrenia that killed him, exactly. He seemed to recover but kept having relapses. And the muscular rigidity of his hands and fingers from the medications made it more and more frustrating to play the piano.

"All he would eat was brown rice and watermelon, and he refused to put his food in the refrigerator. So we weren't surprised when he got sick and didn't get him to the hospital until it was too late to stop the hemorrhaging. They think it was an ulcer."

I responded carefully, probing for more revelations in my family story. "I know my mother told me my father was paranoid schizophrenic. But she said he refused treatment, and it sounded like after the divorce he was OK."

Mori reached for her tea, moving cautiously to keep from straining her incision. "Oh, well, I never did know what was wrong with your father, he was never really normal, you know. I think he had bad genes, that really came out in Paul. And it sounds like your brother Corwin got a touch of it, too. But that's why I realized I should tell you about Paul, so you can watch your son. And let your children know, in case they have children."

I couldn't think about this anymore, couldn't react yet. "Right. You must be tired. Do you want a nap, or some lunch first?"

* * *

When I first visited her the Christmas after Daddy died, Mori had shared many memories of Paul. As she took me room by room through their large Victorian house, she apologized that she had lost interest in housekeeping when Paul died. Food preparation areas in the kitchen were spotless, but otherwise, the house was piled with papers, household objects, memorabilia, and with fourteen years worth of dust. The dining room table was covered with Paul's music, notices of his memorial service, and cards and letters of condolence. Many of the cards had been torn in two. "I was angry," Mori explained.

My suitcase had been lost on the plane, so Mori dressed me in her clothes and said I was the daughter she had never had. We sat up late into the nights, drinking tea and eating Clementines, and Mori told me stories of the twenty-five-year family she and my father had had with Paul. She spoke Paul's name with adoration as she chronicled his life. Their only child, Paul had always been serious and intense, like a little adult, not childish. As a young child he was obsessed with brushes, then machines, then robots. When he discovered music, they bought him a toy piano, and soon found he could play by ear anything he heard. On vacation in Zurich when he was twelve, they lost him one day, and finally found him in the hotel bar, as close as he could get to the piano, listening and talking to the pianist.

Mori and I went to Clark's Pond, behind the house in Bloomfield where first I, then Paul, spent our early childhood years. We scattered some of my father's ashes on the pond, and Mori recited the invocation "To God" she had first said when they scattered Paul's ashes there:

"As he was not lost to you in giving,

So he is not lost to us in giving back.

"What we sometimes call Death is only a horizon.

And a horizon is nothing but the limit of our sight.

Where others are, and Thou art, we, too, will be."

***

Over the next eight years, I would return numerous times,

by day retracing the steps of my New Jersey family, by night assimilating the history with Mori over tea. We went into the City for jazz concerts by Barry Harris, who had been Paul's teacher. During high school, Paul had started studying jazz with Barry Harris in New York, taking the bus in from New Jersey several nights a week, and on weekends. When he graduated, his studies became full-time, and his parents encouraged him because he showed such talent and promise.

On one of my visits, we were invited to a rehearsal of Barry's group, and Mori introduced me to Barry. His studio was on East 7th Street, across from Tompkins Square Park in the East Village, where I had hung out as an NYU student/hippie in the late '60s. Barry took my hand gravely, almost reverently, "Your brother was a fine musician, and Mori is a very special lady. I'm pleased you and she have each other now."

* * *

Inevitably, being back at my two former homes brought up fantasies:

I was almost fifteen, Paul was three, and they had just moved to the big house in Glen Ridge. Eight years after their divorce, my mother had finally allowed me to visit my father, because he had a wife and child now and seemed relatively stable. The commuter train speeding through the gully across the street shook us awake each morning. I would hurry downstairs to have breakfast with Daddy when he got home from his night shift at the printing company in the City. He would let me have coffee mixed half and half with milk, and I felt very grown-up and special compared to little Paul. I wasn't very interested in little children, and Paul didn't have much use for me, but we got along.

After breakfast, Daddy went upstairs to sleep and Mori sent us out to the sunny front porch, where Paul played silently with his toy robot and I read my book. I could hardly wait for the weekend when Daddy was taking me to New York for a matinee of **The Sound of Music**, *just him and me....*

Fast forward four years:

I was settled in the East Village with my first live-in boyfriend, Bear, and was starting at NYU. I had met Daddy for lunch in the spring when I came to the SE Bronx for VISTA volunteer training, and he was excited that I was going to be living in the City for a few years. I was nervous at first when he showed up unannounced at our 4th-floor walk-up on East Tenth Street (we didn't have a telephone). Daddy seemed alarmed himself at first by our bare-bones railroad flat, with no furniture but a mattress in the living room. Then he noticed a copy of <u>Remembrance of Things Past</u> by the bathtub in the kitchen. Soon he and Bear were deep in conversation about Proust and their mutual love of literature. (I didn't have the heart to tell him I had been the one spending the summer in the bathtub reading Proust.)

Daddy invited us to come to New Jersey to see his collection of James Joyce's first editions. We took the bus over from Port Authority the next Saturday. Paul, a little man at 7 years old now, played Mozart on his keyboard for us. Daddy showed us copies of the science fiction magazine he published when he was in high school. Bear, a recent philosophy graduate student from Stanford, was duly impressed and fit right in. I was light-headed with the sophistication of my "other family." It must have been my mother's Southern ignorance that had made her think my father was crazy!

In reality, I had had no contact with my father or his new family from my parent's divorce when I was seven years old until I was fifty. I received birthday and Christmas cards, signed only, "Love, Daddy" and an occasional present. My numerous letters to him were never acknowledged. My mother, crying, had told me that my father was a paranoid schizophrenic, that he had remarried and had a son named Paul, but nothing more. I knew better than to ask.

My boyfriend Bear had told me once when we lived on East Tenth Street that he saw a man looking at our mailboxes and thought it was my father. I couldn't believe him, didn't even write to my father for the three years I lived so close to him. Sure enough, Mori's stories of my father confirmed this incident. Daddy had found my apartment in the East Village but "lost his nerve" to knock on the door.

* * *

After the initial shock of Mori's revelation about Paul's illness, I was eager to hear the whole story, and Mori overflowed with details. Her stories ran the gamut from funny scenes to painful accounts of their struggles with Paul's treatments and relapses.

At first Paul's delusions and paranoia seemed to be adolescent rebellion against his parents, and they encouraged him to get out on his own. He moved to Boston but got involved there with a group of young people dedicated to macrobiotics and meditation. He became, as Mori put it, "one of the people wearing orange robes and chanting 'Hare Krishna' at airports."

"How did you figure out whether he had just joined a cult or become mentally ill?" I asked Mori. This was feeling all too familiar: my husband Pat had become involved with a cult that turned into a folie -a -deux with his guru, before Pat's brain tumor was discovered. And my father's apparent schizophrenic episode had developed from his obsession with science fiction.

"Well, his grandmother died, whom he'd always been so close to, and then he met a girl in Boston and got into some kind of disastrous relationship. He got kicked out of his community, and really went downhill.

"We got a telephone call from his landlord saying he was putting Paul on the next train home. Then we took him to a psychologist and two psychiatrists, who all said, "Very serious." He spent seventeen days in Roosevelt Hospital and lost all his hallucinations. But he progressed so rapidly—too rapidly—that he was off his medications within a few months."

"But he stayed at home after that, and you took care of him?" I asked, looking for the happy ending, of sorts, before the medical fluke that ended Paul's life.

"Well we tried to take care of him. He wanted to do it on his own, but he wasn't able to keep things straight if I didn't go to his appointments with him.

"I remember once Paul and I were arguing walking cross-town to Port Authority after an appointment with his psychiatrist. He started walking ahead of me, turning back every minute or so to scream at me. And it was almost funny how the crowds parted for us like the Red Sea parted for Moses….. It was almost funny." Mori mused.

"I know," I responded, "Pat and I had a similar scene walking up Broadway, in Seattle, after his brain surgery. He fell in the street, and the pedestrians all moved back as if nothing was happening, while I helped him up. And Pat said, "That was so embarrassing, I'm never going to let that happen to me again!'"

Mori continued, "Paul got really frustrated and depressed. He tried to get back into his music and made some money playing at a couple of local restaurants. But he hated being dependent on his parents, and he kept having relapses…."

More material for my fantasy connections with Paul:

In 1981 I was married, living in Seattle, with two small children and a home daycare. Paul got out of the hospital with his new schizophrenia diagnosis, and Daddy asked if he could come spend some time with his big sister. Paul was excited about the jazz scene in Seattle and didn't mind sleeping on the couch in our cramped apartment in the Central District. Pat took him under his wing, took him to the Blue Moon, and introduced him around. Paul started to hang out with Robert Cray and Tim Scott at Jackson Street After Hours. Soon he was closing the clubs every night, then catching a few hours of sleep on the couch until my daycare kids arrived. He was shy with the children, but sweet, and played little songs for them on his keyboard. But Pat and I were in survival mode ourselves, and when the rain started in the fall the apartment was too full to hold us all. Paul went back to New Jersey and never made it back.

I felt a strange familiarity with this brother I never met.

My marriage had ended with my husband's psychosis, as had my mother's. Yet Mori and I had each found a way to have reasonably normal lives with these damaged men. Now we could share the love, sadness, and dark humor

that had carried us through.

When Mori died, it fell to me to sort through her possessions and papers.

I found a trove of photographs and letters about Paul, and his drawings and music tapes. Halloween photos showed his progression from dressing up as a teabag to a series of robot costumes. Christmas photos showed him meeting his new life-sized toy robots as if they were new friends. Adolescence brought stylized drawings of robotic people, and photographs of Paul with his keyboard, headphones, and tape players. In photos with Barry Harris, Paul and his fellow students crowded around Barry's piano, intent on the music and Barry's hands on the keyboard. I found a photo of my father cradling baby Paul and sobbed. I should have been there, next to Paul if not in his place.

I found the draft of a letter Mori had written, "History of Paul Stickney, 22 years":

> *Paul was born in July 1959, immediately finding the physical world a comfortable and enjoyable place to be. As a baby he studied everything intently and seriously, and was alert and well-coordinated….at 3, he had a vocabulary well beyond his years….Before age 2 Paul had a very long attention span. He could spend hours at one activity while other children ran around doing many things. He could draw in minute detail with a ballpoint pen at 2 and preferred toys with many details to simple shaped ones. He tended to relate to adults rather than to his peers, and liked a great deal of time alone to play, concentrating deeply….*
>
> *Paul's life has been a series of passionate interests which he has devoted himself to almost exclusively: 18 mos. – 2 years, brushes; 2 – 4, construction equipment machines (toys and real ones to watch and sit in); 4 – 8, robots (toys and TV programs); 8 – 10, chemistry and elements, formulas, and tables; 11 – 16 music (elec. guitar, elec. organ, piano). Music had turned out to be the deepest passion of all, but at 15 he attended a class in macrobiotic cooking & philosophy & went as intensely into that….*

This has to be an Asperger's child! I packed Paul's things separately to ship back to Seattle. I made a collage of his childhood photos with robots for my office bulletin board, my teaching display about autism.

"What got you interested in Asperger's and schizophrenia?" my coworkers and clients ask. We are attracted to the familiar. The familiar which was lost has a stronger, haunting attraction.

"I had a brother…"

TRAPPED

THIS YEAR, WITH THE PANDEMIC, I'm homebound for the first time since childhood. My world in Olympia has shrunk. Bob has always wanted me to be home more, but I had work, meetings, shopping, and errands. Now there's nowhere to go. The days wash together like watercolors. I feel like I'm stuck in the movie Groundhog Day. The same pills in the same order every morning, every night.

Sometimes I have to feel my washcloth to remember if I washed my face. I deliberately vary my bath days, cooking days, and online shopping days. Singing my preschool song, "Today is Monday, Monday, Monday, that's today." Determined to remember even when it makes no difference. My activities focus around the internet, TV news, doing online counseling, and Zoom meetings.

I finish each day by checking my list, highlighting what to do first tomorrow. Reading in bed every night, the same quick goodnight kiss. Bob says he's glad I'm home, but wishes I didn't always want to be doing something!

I push the snooze alarm in the morning to turn onto my stomach and stretch, for two or three ten-minute cycles. To get up, I think only about having my cup of coffee. Then, I can look at my list of tasks for another day. "Here comes another one, just like the other one..."

I have a new sense of the shape of my life. With the pandemic, suddenly I'm old. What if this is the end—what if I have to stay home the rest of my life? Terrifying idea! I still live *in medias res*. I'm not ready to put my affairs in order or to do a life review.

So many of the important people in my life are dead now. Dreams twist with memories. They're episodes, whole little worlds that open and close, then I remember another.

One morning I wake up reciting my former husband's social security number, over and over. He died in 1998.

Poems I learned in school come back to me, while words I need day-to-day leave me, leaving holes. It takes so much energy to stay in this new, current reality!

Zoom gives me a new lens for connections—with work, with Black Lives Matter and the horrors of what our country has become. But push the button and it snaps shut. The people on the call I feel so connected with are suddenly gone. My young video-therapy clients know the power of being "the one to push the button."

By May, I hunger for the real world. I start taking a walk every evening, in the neighborhood, walking further each time, in concentric circles. I learn to know each house, each tree, and the flowers, and to marvel at their beauty and their brightness. I am reminded of a poem I memorized in eighth grade, by Gerard Manley Hopkins:

Pied Beauty
Glory be to God for dappled things--
For skies of couple-colour as a brinded cow;.
For rose-moles all in stipple upon trout that swim...

Occasionally I see people in their yards and cross to the other side of the street. I notice how many are people of color, and how immaculate most of the houses and yards are. I give them names, and make up little stories about them.

When the days start getting shorter again, the rhythm of my walks is broken. We move into Phase 3 of the stay-at-home orders. I go some places and nothing happens, so I open up my routines a bit.

When I start spending Wednesday afternoons with my granddaughter Twana in her backyard, my hope comes back.

Twana is eight years old, a tall, graceful Skokomish and Makah Native child with long black hair. When the pandemic began, she stopped wearing shoes, indoors and out. She and a few friends are allowed to play together outside, six feet apart, and they run all over their cul-de-sac neighborhood—climbing trees, tracking fairies in the woods, choreographing dances on the lawns. She and I choose a different craft project each Wednesday—making Japanese lanterns for Hiroshima Day, picking blackberries and making jam, gluing together popsicle sticks to make fairy houses.

I tell Twana stories about my own childhood in Arkansas. I never had shoes in the summer, I had a place in my grandmother's magnolia tree to read in the hot afternoons, I spent hours weaving potholders. I find the same simple loom with loops on Amazon and order it for Twana.

I grew up in a simpler world than this one.

The summer I was ten, Don gave me a broken heart necklace. I was in the backyard at home making mudpies. He rode up on his bike and leaned over the low chickenwire fence, handing me a necklace and saying, "Here, Jean, I brought you a broken heart."

There were seven boys and seven girls in our seventh-grade class, and we were the last to pair up. I don't remember that we ever went anywhere together, or kissed, or even held hands, but we never broke up, either. He just told me he needed to spend more time with his horse.

The rest of that summer I rode my bike over to Aunt Mildred's house every morning, because Don lived next door to her, and I might catch a glimpse of him. Aunt Mildred was always busy, and I never liked her anyway, but her maid would give me an ice-cold Coca-Cola. I sat by the kitchen counter on a stool to drink it — delicious because forbidden. I was allowed to drink one Coke a day, in the afternoon, no more. And Mother and Mamoe would have scolded me if they knew, for imposing on Aunt Mildred like this, despite her being the richest woman in Texarkana.

Summers were endless as I grew into my teens. I was supposed to go to the Country Club to swim and play golf with Mamoe's friends' grandchildren, but they were all mean to me. I stayed home and read, and wove potholders. Sometimes Mamoe would tell me to pick up pecans from the big tree in her backyard and crack them. I didn't mind, because I could eat the broken parts, and most of them broke if I turned the nutcracker too tight.

One summer I took a sewing class and used Mamoe's treadle sewing machine to make clothes to wear to high school. I liked choosing the patterns and the fabric, but they were strange clothes, not the Liz Taylor blouses with ruffles around the hips that the popular girls wore. Another summer I wanted to learn to knit, so every day after lunch my mother dropped me off at an old house that was a knitting shop. I sat on the porch rocking and knitting with women sixty years older than me. The woman who knitted left-handed took a fancy to me, also a lefty, and helped me. Later I found out that no one knits left-handed, so no one else could ever help me.

Once I could drive, at sixteen, summers were harder, not easier. The summer before college, I wanted to go out every night, but I always had to come up with a reason. To go over to Ruth's house, or Catherine's house, or to the post office to mail a letter.

"I can always mail it for you on my way to work in the morning, Jean," Mother would say. I couldn't tell her that I felt trapped—not anxious really, just needing to get out of the house. Mother never said no. Worse, she asked, "Why?" or said, "I wish you didn't want that." I was just sixteen, but it was time for me to move away from home!

That summer was the end of my being homebound—at least until now.

SAVE AS

THE NEUROSCIENTISTS nowadays
say, "Memory is not a read-only function."
Good news! I was thinking I would have to
delete the batch of painful memories overloading
my brain, or my head would explode.
Maybe I can modify and save them.
"'The Past' already exists."
"Do you want to replace it?"

My head bursts with ghosts, unable to rest,
their business unfinished.
The father who never looked for me.
The brother I never knew.
The grandmother who sent me outside
to "pick your own switch."
I grew up in spite of them,
but still they haunt me.

My father kept my picture in his wallet.
I inherited my brother's drawings and piano tapes.
My cousins tell stories of fun with
their feisty great-aunt.

I rewrite my memories, fill out the characters,
add my prayers for forgiveness.
They did their best, they loved me in their fashion,
and I can save these edited memories,
and live on.

DAN JORGENSEN

Stories, a memory, and a letter

FRANCIS

10-24-15

This was written for Keith Eisner's class. I had to come up with some writing for the following week and had no idea what to write. I looked out over Puget Sound's foggy view of Vashon Island, and this story developed.

FRANCIS WAS NOT MUCH TO LOOK AT AT BIRTH, a mere wisp of vapor.

He'd grown into a magnificent, sometimes maleficent fog during the last two decades.

Sometimes he surprised himself with as yet undiscovered powers. Yesterday he drifted through a slash pile of burning tree stumps, from a recent California forest fire. He was able to absorb a huge quantity of smoke and carry it all the way to Vancouver Island. He liked surprising those overly-polite Canadians. They weren't the sharpest knives in the drawer that morning. It was a good two or three hours before they realized the smoke wasn't from their precious island. Hah! He heard practically every resident say, "Are we on fire, hey?"

Francis was currently drifting over the Puget Sound area, looking at autumn. He dampened red maple and yellow liquidambar leaves, and added moisture to the rapidly growing layer of falling tree debris. He fanned the ground gently as he passed through, lifting the smell of fragrant decaying vegetation out of the woods, bringing it into the city. He swirled around morning walkers, watching them lift their noses to sniff the fall air with delight. Memories swirled in their heads, memories of raking lawns blanketed with colorful leaves. A flying leap into the final pile would scatter the leaves back to their original locations. The walkers re-lived pleasant childhood memories, making Francis feel worthwhile.

The novelty of being out and about again was a recent thing to Francis. He'd just de-hibernated from an intermittent summer slumber, having hidden himself in odd, lenticular Mt. Rainier clouds. They were kind of like the geeks of clouds. Because of their patterns and colors, they thought they were something special. Hmphh. Their thinking was all wet. It was a good thing, actually. Without their moisture, Francis would've dried out this last hot summer. He usually hid in a mountain cave, condensing himself into a cool, dark puddle. This year it has been fun watching people doing their summer activities. He saw trees, shrubs, and flowers reach full blossoming and leafing beauty. He'd felt like a vampire up to now, only coming out when the days were growing rapidly darker, colder, and shorter.

Francis thought of the many pleasures he enjoyed.

He liked blowing through downtown Seattle, past fancy shops like Nordstrom's and Neiman-Marcus. There were always good-looking women strutting around them. He'd make himself extra moist before blowing through. The naturally curly-haired would start frizzing, heavy mascara would start to sag, spike heels had less of a purchase on the sidewalk and more of an entertainment value.

Can fog smile? Francis did.

Another of his pleasures was the perverse one of sneaking in just after Saturday morning sunshine had appeared. He'd see people come out in shorts, ready to jog, then turn around and layer fog pants over skintight spandex. Putting an extra layer of clothing over the trim aerobic bodies made them look bulked up, something they studiously avoided. He got a kick out of their annoyance.

Sometimes he'd come in at dusk, arriving just as tourists were trying to navigate the local sights. He could cover the city lights with fog. Nothing would be visible. Then he'd periodically, deliberately, partially clear. The oohs and ahhs were rewarding, as the lights became visible. He could make himself so dense that eight foot tall street signs couldn't be read unless a person climbed the sign pole. Now that was funny.

Francis sighed, his gust blowing fancy flowered hats from the heads of well-dressed women and flamboyant men.

He looked forward to Halloween. He liked to soak paper-costumed children, making the paper dye run into their clothes and drip on the sidewalk. He'd hover around candle-lit pumpkins, amplifying the pumpkins' evil sneers and wicked smiles, with a golden aura. Heh, heh. How fun it was to be a little mischievous.

Christmas brought out Francis's goodness. He brought the log-burning-in-the-fireplace smoke to ground level from chimney tops. The fragrance of the log smoke added to the ambiance of Christmas, especially when coupled with Christmas carols and holiday lights. The fog softened and spread the glow of red and green lights, but blue worked okay too. He notice mittened and scarved lovers walk hand-in-hand while admiring his handiwork, even though their eyes were filled mainly with one another. He gave them a soft silence and privacy.

Francis blew into the Des Moines marina Sunday morning. He saw clouds forming above him. It was a good trick, fogging out an area just before the rain came in. Instead of the sky clearing, thunderclouds took over. He liked being the only moisture provider, but clouds sprinkling through him was okay too.

As he stretched out over the marina, he looked into the condo windows. In one of them was a wanna-be writer. The writer had all the appearance of suffering writer's block. His blank face was watching loaded ships being led through the channel by tugboats. Vashon Island was barely visible. The majority of the scenery was blanketed by Francis's formidable fog. The writer was having a mental fog, something Francis couldn't really relate to. It was difficult to understand why someone would choose to stay inside and stress over assignments when he could be out walking in the woods, biking down dirt trails, or doing home improvement projects. But what could a fog know about that?

He swooshed on past the window. He'd look for his friend, Joe. He remembered the morning he'd first met Joe. Francis had been fogging the bay densely enough for crew boat practice to cancel. He'd heard a two person conversation coming from some trees by the Swantown marina. Investigation showed the conversation was coming from only one person, Joe. Joe's appearance inspired Francis to compose some lyrics:
Boogers hanging from his nose
Dirty fingernails pulling up his hose
Steam rising from tattered damp clothes
Periodic shivers racked his old frame
Pretty pathetic and not quite sane.

Francis hung around to listen to Joe.
Joe was babbling:
"...my worthless family. Why did they leave? Because you're a nutcase. I'm just changing right now. I loved being a fish last night in my dreams. See? You're a nutcase. No, I just think I was a fish in a previous life. Yeah right. Maybe I'll be a fish in my next life? Maybe it's because I'm a Pisces? No, it's because you need help. I don't need no help. What about all that seaweed in your pockets then? It is reassuring to me, the feel of the seaweed. It keeps me from panicking when I'm too far away from the water. What about when you smell the beached jellyfish? They smell like the ocean and I like feeling their clear slimy bodies. I get the same feeling in my head when I taste oysters. I feel like I'm sitting on the ocean floor looking up at the surface. Mermaids surround me. You need help, buddy..."

Joe suddenly became aware of Francis. He looked right at the densest part of Francis and introduced himself, "Hi, Mr. Fog, I'm Joe." Francis made himself drizzly wet and blew him a "Glad to meet you, my name is Francis." Joe gave him a toothless grin. Ever since then, they'd been friends.

Joe was bound to be outside by the Sound somewhere. Hard to say where he was. After all, Joe was homeless and could camp wherever he chose. Francis swooshed past Artesian Park, actually a mural-decorated, user-unfriendly paved area. Not there. The Food Bank area was next. Lots of trash, sleeping bags, and portable furniture, but no obvious signs of Joe. Francis looked for a wet, open area, with pieces of seaweed or algae strewn around. They'd be remnants of Joe's spending the night.

Joe, Francis had overheard, had been diagnosed with PFFD (Penchant For Fog & Dampness) and AA (Altogether Awful) last week. He'd seen Joe shake off the diagnoses, but they proved to be discouraging ones for his social worker, Sandy, to deal with. Sandy had been raised in Arizona. "Who the hell would want to be damp all the time?" Sandy said aloud to himself. "I cannot relate to this odder-than-usual-Olympia character." Sandy abandoned Joe, and tended to the nose-ringed, enlarged earlobe, pink and green-haired, multi-dogged homeless instead.

Francis checked Capitol Lake, the tracks of a railroad remnant on the west side, underneath the bridges. No sign of him. None of his fancy, block-lettered, green-inked signs around abandoned in his usual panhandling locations, either. What the hell?

Then Francis remembered seeing dozens of volunteers picking up trash on the Priest Point and Boston Harbor beaches last weekend. Dumpsters had been put out for the clean-up effort. They were dumpsters to everyone but Joe. To him, they were campers. Francis blew himself to the beaches. All but one of the campers had been picked up for dumping. Sure enough, Joe was climbing out of the last one, talking to himself. He was covered with algae and seaweed.

He was babbling, "Yesterday, man what a day. I ain't gonna buy no more of that St. Pauli Girl, N. A. stuff. I wasted my day's earnings on that ale. I drank the whole case and no buzz. You dumb jerk. That's what happens when you buy the beer just because of the buxom German girl on the label. Just 'cause Sandy drinks it doesn't mean it's worthwhile. Yeah, maybe you're right. And another thing, stay away from that fiery tequila. Old Dreadlocks, that pathetic beggar you was panhandling with, gave you half his bottle. Holy Cow, now there was a drink with a bite! Yeah, well you slid into the goddamn lake and passed out!"

Joe had slept comfortably in the dampness and fragrance of his muddy lakeshore nest last night. Sweet dreams of swimming in a school of fish had entertained him. This morning, way hung over, he'd managed to climb the slippery bank of the lake and set up on the roadway from where he'd slid. He had slime hanging from every part of his body. He suspected he looked similar to the Creature from the Black Lagoon. He didn't even have a begging sign filled with nonsensical printing, circles, arrows, God BleSs, heart pictures, WiLL work for Cigars or anything. Maybe his timing was perfect though. It was close to Halloween. Amazingly, there had been an almost unending line of cars, driven by looky-loos. They wanted to donate something as payment for the eye candy. No one stopped, but donations had been thrown through the passenger windows. Money, old tomatoes, a dirty Dodgers ball cap, some green Leggos, a starter from a Kenworth, a couple half-smoked Cuban stogies, and a Barry Manilow LP. Friendly finger gestures were also given to him when he fell off the curb into traffic. The treasures had piled up on his feet as he tried to clean the gunk from his face. A reporter from *The Olympian* stopped to interview him, or did he? Hard to remember now. He remembered the click of a camera shutter dozens of times, but he didn't remember actually answering any questions. The cops eventually scooped him up. They dressed in disposable white tyvek suits and gloves. They drove him to a dumpster near Boston Harbor after bagging all his goodies. They dropped the treasures with him. Joe appreciated it.

Joe was removing sea debris and flotsam from his well-broken-in homeless suit when Francis gave him an affectionate, wet "Good morning, buddy."

"Hiya," Joe said. "How they hangin'? Ha Ha. What a joker I am. Why doesn't Sandy realize how lucky he is to have me as a client, a multi-personalitied, colorful, good-natured, very portable gentleman?"

Francis, having found Joe, settled down for a while. He

was hoping for a new soliloquy or an odd poem on a new panhandling sign. Last week Joe's sign had been,
Slime it is
Slimy I be
But feast your eyes
On what you see.
Kick me a dollar
A cigar perhaps
You'll see this beggar
Do a Bojangles dance!

Joe started singing, "I wish I was an Oscar Meyer Wiener, That is what I truly wish to be, 'Cause if I was an Oscar Meyer Wiener, Everyone would be in love with me."

It was over the top for Francis. A morning hot dog song was unpalatable, even for his foggy personality. He whooshed off to find other entertainment.

Despite the enthusiastic fogginess of Francis, the sunshine was starting to penetrate him into the bay. Francis started to condense himself hurriedly. He found a large, mostly covered culvert to drip his wet presence into. The last few drops of fog dripped through the blackberry-covered grate as Francis drifted off, to sleep through the autumn day. Maybe he'd find Joe again later. Maybe the sun would just stay out forever and ever, giving him fog block. Don't worry about it right now.

Maybe, maybe, maybe… Wet, soft snores were audible from the culvert.

FATHER'S DAY

June, 2020

Dad did not show affection easily and was difficult to live with. He was a good provider though, and meant well.

Dad, English Teacher
At work and home.
Spelling, grammar, punctuation
Frequently interrupted conversation
During most dinners.
Seldom asked was:
Have fun today?
Any exciting events?
Win at marbles?
Any new friends?

A penalty box
Graced the table.
If we spoke
Overused words like
Good, nice, pretty,
We were forced
To contribute to it.
It seemed like
We couldn't describe

Our school day
Without incurring penalty,
And forfeiting allowance.
Now in adulthood,
Vocabulary, spelling, pronunciation
Have benefited me.

Dad's attitude changed
In his 60's.
We three kids
Did not visit.
Why would we?
He became our friend.
He helped buy
My first house,
Backpacked with me,
Replaced a broken washer,
When affordability was an issue for me.

Stroke at 75
Put him into
An irreversible coma.
Mom, my sister,
And I each took
8 hour watches
By his bedside.
I read <u>Lonesome Dove</u> to him,
On my shift.
Changes in breathing

Could be heard
When I read dodgy parts.
His final inhalation
During my shift.
He passed quietly.
I love you, Dad.

DEAR SIDNE

May 2020
A letter to my older sister, after a negative critique from her.

WOULD YOU LIKE TO KNOW why I care that your critique of my recent story hurt me more than anyone else's critique did?

Let's see, it all began when we were kids.

Your girlfriends were very cute, and I was shy. It was such a luxury seeing beautiful girls in my own house!

If something of yours broke, and I was able to repair it for you, I was always more than happy to do it.

You were the first one to escape Dad's influence when I was so desperately unhappy at home because of him. I admit, since I was a teenager and historically prone to be unhappy, Dad was not the exclusive cause.

You started to listen to Rock 'n' Roll around 1966. I loved it. Finally a change from that horrible classical that I was so incredibly tired of. I started loving Rock 'n' Roll that year because of you.

I remember when you started driving the 1959 pastel yellow Ford station wagon. You drove with your knees while ratting your hair. I was amazed that someone could do that!

The paintings and sculptures you made, in your classes at California State University, Santa Barbara were wonderful. The bright colors, the occasional nude. I liked your sculptures perhaps because I'd never done anything like that, but probably because anything you did was okay with me.

Your selections of jazz I'd never heard, broadened my horizons and made me realize that I liked jazz too, even if it was only the jazzy parts of Carole King and James Taylor.

Visiting you, when you switched to Cal Berkeley, was a real

eye-opener for me. People's Park, a Joan Baez concert, stores I'd never seen in Fresno, and the atmosphere of that anything-can-happen town. Very exciting.

When Jeanne and I came to visit you, after you moved to San Francisco, you let us sleep together in your living room. I remember the blanket you made with cowhide and fur. Way cool. The four of us would pile into your Dodge Dart, with the push-button transmission. (Husband) Buff would tune to a reggae or rap station, put the convertible top down, and we'd sail through the S.F. streets, all of us singing, hooting, hollering, especially Buff, smiling at the ridiculous fun of it, the wind whizzing by our heads, the ocean visible at the tops of the hills. At night we'd walk downhill to Uncle's Cafe and eat Chinese food in an exotically decorated and crowded Chinatown.

You divorced and remarried and moved to Santa Rosa. (Husband) Blaine was working as a recreation director for a wealthy retirement community. His annual Hawaiian pig roast will never be forgotten. Mouth-watering fabulous. Your friends, V &P were always entertaining when they got drunk. She was so cute.

Something was always going on, a party, a trip for you to China, or other foreign destination, to arrange an international child adoption. The whole adoption scenario was unspeakably complex and intimidating to me.

I also thought it was amazing that you two lived in England, where your first child was born. Your life was so busy and complex. I don't think I could've done anything like that.

I forgot to mention that I thought it was so cool when you were living in Alaska, doing a disc jockey job.

You have done so much with your life that I would never think of doing. I was trying to figure out how to put food on the table, when I married at age 25, didn't know what I wanted to do as a vocation, and attended Cal State Fresno for a Bachelor's degree. I was learning how to be a dad too. Life was not boring, it was one crisis after another.

The work at Caltrans was the most challenging work I had

ever done. I wasn't even aware I was smart enough to do it. Somehow I put in 22 years and got out of the rat race before I self-destructed.

Two tumor surgeries, a heart surgery, a divorce, a geographical relocation, another marriage, a real estate purchase later, here I am.

I started trying to write when I wanted to entertain my new love, long distance. I also stopped drinking to promote her affection. She ended our romance, but I'm still writing and a year sober.

The reason I'm writing this note to you is to tell you that you have been the greatest influence in practically all aspects of my life. I didn't look up to Dad, Mom was my friend, and my brother was always on a different wavelength, but I figured I could try to imitate your life, and hopefully, my life would work out.

Apparently, you will be forever stuck with me as one of your fans. I hope you know that I'm putting the pressure on you, now that I've told you my secret.

Bye.

Love, Dan

ONE DAY AT THE HOME
November 2019

Mom was in a home for the last 2-3 years of her life. Her Alzheimers made each visit a surprise. This was one such visit...or was it?

WEDNESDAY. TIME FOR AN AA MEETING, 45-minute walk on the Sound, coffee with a friend at Bread Peddler, then a Mom visit.

I ring the doorbell and a caregiver lets me inside. I find Mom in her usual place on the couch. She is wearing old blue slacks, a white ruffled blouse, and turquoise socks with animal patterns. She is slumped to one side, slack-jawed and half-asleep, in front of an inane tv game show.

"Hi honey," she says. My hair has been washed two days in a row!"

"Really?" I say.

"Hey Mom, what about taking a ride?"

I transfer Mom from the couch to her wheelchair. She is ready to go outside on this warm, late fall day.

"Have you seen my house in the woods?" Mom asks me, as we roll over a carpet of bright orange and yellow leaves. They cover sidewalk bumps and holes.

"Ahhh!" she bursts out, as I hit a bump with the wheelchair.

"Where exactly is it, Mom?" I ask her.

"I don't remember," she replies.

"Maybe we'll come across it," I say, as we continue our walk, passing two or three unimproved, tree-filled lots.

Mom has repeatedly asked me, on previous walks, if I've seen the chicken wire house that she built in someone's yard. She doesn't remember where it is. I reassure her, on every visit, that maybe one day we'll discover it. The house in the woods is a new variation of the same theme.

We roll along, stopping to retrieve a red leaf that Mom considers worth keeping. I stop when she points out a strikingly bright yellow dandelion flower that she'd like me to pick.

I stop to pick the bloom for her. It is down a slope, on the edge of a wooded area. I am plucking the flower when I hear a leaf-crunching noise. I turn to see Mom's wheelchair start to roll over the edge of the sidewalk and head downhill. I must have forgotten to lock the wheels!

"Oh crap!" I yell as the wheelchair hurtles toward me. I am unable to stop it. I'm thrown to one side. Mom's face is beaming as she breaks land speed records for hurtling wheelchairs. I am half-expecting to hear a sonic boom.

She miraculously stays seated in the chair, despite the fact that she has no seat belt, and sits in a leaning-to-the-left fashion. Mom hurtles through low underbrush, winding her way past Oregon Grape bushes and young, thin, yellow-leaved Poplar trees. I have no idea what guides her. Must be an unseen heavenly force or Mom's power of thought control.

I pick myself up, brushing debris and dirt from my clothing. She disappears from sight. I follow the path of broken foliage. The hill loses much of its slope after the first 300 feet and the chair finally rolls to a stop. Mom is still in it. Her gray hair is wild-looking. It has sticks and yellow leaves poking out. The bushes have whisked off her red Hawaiian ball cap. She's wearing a huge grin. She's parked on what appears to be a one-foot-wide trail.

"Are you okay, Mom?" I ask.

"This is it!" she blurts out. "This is the path to my house."

I look down the trail. It meanders another hundred feet or so. The branches of the trees make a twilight tunnel, ending at what looks like some sort of shingled structure. The building has a soft, surreal glow to it. Outside lights on each side of the door flicker.

The wheelchair is too wide to go any farther. I disconnect Mom's oxygen, pick her up, and carry her to the building. I ease her down into a tall pile of leaves in front of the cottage and lean her against a tree.

Above the door is an artistically made redwood sign. It reads, *Ruthie's House In The Woods.* Of course it reads that, I think. What else would I expect? The top of the doorway is maybe five feet tall. I hear music playing inside. It sounds like *Moonlight Serenade.* I open the door, made from small moss-covered sticks lashed together, with rawhide shoe laces as hinges.

A table of a ragged piece of plywood, supported by two stumps, sits in the middle of the room. It's set with a white tablecloth, red cloth napkins, white china plates, and silverware. Placards with guests' names are inside small chicken wire houses at each place setting. Champagne glasses etched with *Tom and Ruth* are set around.

I feel a presence behind me. Mom has walked in from the leaf pile. She has a dreamy look on her face. Her hair is freshly brushed. Red lipstick and fresh makeup have been applied. She is wearing a fancy, long, floral-patterned dress from the 1930s and red heels. I can smell Chanel perfume as she passes me. Gads, she is stunning.

Seated at the table, watching Mom make her entrance, are two couples that she and Dad played cards with. At the head of the table is Dad! Mom rushes up to him. Their intimate, desperately joyous hug brings tears to my eyes. The other guests are clapping and whistling.

The one-room cottage is warmed by a popping, crackling fire in a small brick fireplace. The fragrant smell of burning Cedar permeates the air. Multi-colored streamers are stretched in all directions from a central, roof-supporting post. Large branches fan out from the post to support a thatched roof.

Pickled herring, potato chips, avocado dip, sliced oranges, caramel-nut coffee cake, mixed nuts, and almond champagne wait at the table.

I feel invisible. No one in the room appears to have even noticed me. I attempt to let Mom know that I'll return in an hour or so. She doesn't acknowledge me. I leave the cottage as

Chattanooga Choo Choo starts playing and everyone gets up to dance.

I walk out of the woods and back to my truck, still in a daze. I drive home. Two hours later, I return to her group home, ring the doorbell, and am admitted.

Mom is seated in her usual place, at the end of the overstuffed leather couch, leaning to one side. Her oxygen is hooked up. She is blankly staring at the large-screen tv. A 1940s opera is playing.

She turns to me. "Hi honey," she says. She opens her arms for a hug and kiss.

"Hi, Mom. You have quite a bit of color in your cheeks. Have you been doing calisthenics?"

"Maybe," she says. She winks at me and gives me a hint of a smile.

MARTHA ILES WORCESTER

Connecting Old and Young

These stories and one prose poem began with a memory seed and became creative non-fiction. The stories and poem blend together my own past experiences and those of elders and young people I've known in different times and places. As my memories come together in written words, they bloom into parts of who I am and give meaning to my life.

CALL ME MR. GRUMP!

I'VE BEEN IN THIS NURSING HOME for a whole year now. I can hardly believe it! After the fall that broke my hip, I thought I'd get back to normal, back to my farm where I could watch the seasons change and just be left alone; pass into the next life in my recliner, like my wife did. But no, my children, all over sixty-five now, fooled me. Told me I'd only be here a week or two after my hip surgery. But now I know I'll never leave this place.

My back is so bent, I can't stand up straight. I have to use a walker to get across the room or I'll fall on my face. Here I am at 98 stuck in this nursing home. Everyone treats me like a child with no past and no brain. Most people here think I'm some weak old sick man that needs prodding to eat, to move, to do whatever they ask at whatever hour they want it to happen.

I'm not as weak as they think. Ha! I can hold my own. I learned early on that when I'm angry, it scares them and they leave me alone, giving me some peace and quiet. That's all I really want now. They've even given up making me eat in the dining room.

When I first came, I asked nicely if I could eat in my room. They didn't listen, ignored my words. They'd lift me out of my bed, set me in my wheelchair, and roll me into the dining room. They'd hover over me, try to get me to eat everything on my plate, talk to me like a two-year-old. But if I started cursing loudly, they'd take me back to my room. After a couple months, they finally let me eat in my room. I tell you, when they bring my meal, I don't touch a thing until they leave. They call me Mr. Grump and I don't mind. It makes people keep their distance. They never pronounce my name right anyway!

I am so tired after all those years of farm work. Had to add on a tractor repair business to keep enough money coming in for me and my wife. Her health slowly got worse. She died at home in her recliner sitting by me, gasping as she took her last breaths. I felt helpless to do anything but watch her go. I didn't call 911. It was her request. I honored it…it was hard.

I closed her eyes and called her doctor to tell him she'd passed. He said, "I'll come right out" and he did. Couldn't believe it! But what a blessing he did. Took care of all the details of getting her body out of the house and told me what a good job I'd done caring for her. He'd been our family doctor for a long time. He'd made sure our oldest son, Jason, had the best medical care.

Jason *(sigh)*, all those years he had to live with the mind of a five-year-old. He died when he was only 50. We were relieved to see him go, but we all learned a lot of patience from him. His younger brothers helped care for him. I made sure they treated him right.

So now? I've made my peace with the world. The only thing I haven't figured out is how to get my son to quit coming to see me. He comes most every day, insists I get up, use my walker, and go down the hall once or twice with him. That's the only time I leave my room. It hurts so much to move. The only way I can make myself do it is to curse with each step. I know his heart is good. He thinks he's helping me out, keeping me moving. As if I need to move anymore. Wish he'd just let me go like I let my wife go. I begged him not to come, but I finally quit begging. He'd look so hurt like I didn't love him. And it didn't work anyway. He's had a pretty rough life himself, and he did a lot to help me care for Jason. It's the one thing I can do for him, get up and walk. But damn, the pain is awful! And I'm not about to take those pain pills the nurses keep offering me. They make my mind feel like mush. It's enough not to have my body work like I want it to.

They all think I'm a mean angry person with not much mind left, but I'm all here, just in a lot of pain when I walk. I'm glad to be left alone. But then… there's that night-aid, Wendy. She makes my day, or should I say makes my night *(laughs)*. Wendy comes in when she has a bit of free time and sings to me, seems to know I enjoy it. Other nights she'll sit and tell me about how hard it is to raise her son, Jamie, and work nights. Sometimes I tell her a bit about my Jason, and she smiles. When she's in the room, I forget my old aching body. She doesn't ask me to do anything!

   Some days I try to figure out how to do myself in, but that takes more figuring than I've got the strength to do. The time passes. I lose myself in memories.

   Last night I was falling asleep, and it crossed my mind, I hadn't seen Wendy in over a week. She'd probably gotten better work. Drifting off, I thought I saw her at the door but decided I was dreaming.

   Then, there she was sitting by my bed.
   She touched my hand
      Jamie's been sick. But he's better now.
       I hoped you'd still be here.
   And she began to sing.

SOFTENING SORROW

JENNY'S MOTHER SAID the night before, "No school tomorrow, you can sleep late."
The sun's bright light shining on Jenny's bed begged her to get up. It was 10 0'clock, the first Monday after school ended for the summer. She dressed quickly, found her mother standing at the sink in the kitchen, and announced.

"I'm going outside, Mama."

"Not till you eat something, Honey."

Her mother set a box of cheerios on the table and a small pitcher of milk. Jenny pushed a chair up to the table and climbed onto it. Her legs dangled under the chair. She was shorter than most kids in her class. Impatient to be outside, she set her legs in motion, swinging them back and forth while she spooned cheerios into her mouth. She eyed her mother's back to be sure she wasn't looking before putting her lips to the bowl's rim. She drank the last bit of milk and slid off the chair.

Jenny's mother turned from the sink, collected the bowl and pitcher, and rumpled her daughter's red curly hair. "Okay, you can go out now. Remember, don't go across the street without asking me."

Jenny skipped to the front door and let the screen slam behind her. She sat on the stoop trying to decide what to do next. The dusty pot-holed street in front of the house was empty of cars, as usual. Only a few passed by each day. Pineville, population 3 500, was tucked in among the mountains of Northern California. Seasons there were sharply divided into three months each. Winters held deep snows. Spring thaws arrived on schedule in late March with a profusion of wildflowers. Summers, though hot and dry, were made bearable by mountain breezes. Falls were cool and colorful with leafy deciduous trees blended well among tall pines and long-needled ponderosas.

Jenny and her parents had moved to Pineville at the start of the last school year.

Jenny liked the feel of the warm sun. She stuck her bottom lip out and creased her forehead wishing her classmates were nearby. Most lived too far away for Jenny to go there alone. She had no big brothers or sisters to accompany her. She studied the big gray two-story house across the street and tried to imagine what the rooms were like inside. The lawn was overgrown and uneven with dandelions peeking out here and there. The low fence surrounding the lawn was in disrepair. Leaning fence posts barely supported the large, squared wire fencing, and the boards framing the top sagged. She remembered her mother saying, "Now don't you go bothering that old woman, and don't go across the street without asking me first."

* * *

The old woman was mowing her lawn at the side of the house and came around to mow the lawn in front. Her long white hair streamed down her back. The breeze caught a few strands and blew them crosswise tickling her face. She had oiled the rusty mower blades and connecting points between the wheels and axles the evening before. She was pleased the mower rolled smoothly over the bumpy lawn, leaving a path through the tall grass.

She stopped to straighten her aching back. With one hand on the mower handle to steady her balance, she brushed strands of hair and beads of sweat from her face. She looked at her gray weather-beaten house with the big screened-in porch. None of the original paint remained. The colorless gray was now uniform. Millie argued with herself for the hundredth time, "You should paint it to protect those old boards; but I like the look of it the way it is. The roof needs to be replaced; but it doesn't leak, and it will likely last at least as long as I do."

Glad she had hung onto the house, Millie had returned ten years ago to take up residence. She inherited the house from her parents after their death in an auto accident on her 25th birthday. At the time Millie was working in Chicago for a law firm as a paralegal. Despite all the Pineville house's troublesome renters and fights with the property manager, she was never able to bring herself to sell it.

"Can I really be eighty years old?" Millie wondered how she managed to live through three miscarriages, a failed marriage, and that short liaison with a man she hardly knew. The liaison had resulted in her only daughter. Much about the man had faded from her memory, yet she clearly recalled his displeased look when she told him she was pregnant. He didn't say a word, touched her hair, turned away, and went out the door. He never contacted her again. She became unsure if he'd even given her his right name. She had not asked where he lived or worked and found she had no interest in trying to contact him again. Her paralegal work had taught her the futility and cost of tracking down fathers of children. She found the legal work rewarding and it gave her the security needed for raising her child. Since then, she had not been willing to trust a man enough to love her daughter the way she did.

Half done with mowing the front yard, Millie paused to gather her strength. Her gaze shifted to the child sitting on the stoop across the street. The child had sold her California poppies a few days back. "A penny a piece, she'd said." Millie bought them all. She remembered the freckles sprinkled across the small child's cheeks and nose and thought she must be about five or six years old.

Millie felt tears on her face and a deep ache rising in her chest. She took a deep breath and stood awhile, letting the tears come. Memories flooded in of her daughter Melanie. Tears falling were not a new experience for Millie. She wondered what had brought them on just now. She looked again at the child on the stoop. She didn't look anything like the child she'd lost. She smiled through the tears. She knew. It was the child's posture. Leaning forward with elbows resting on her knees, palms of hands holding up her chin. It was a pose Melanie had often assumed.

Memories of the day Melanie died washed over Millie. She firmed her balance, gripping the lawn mower handle with one hand while raising her other arm to wipe tears from her face and chin. Though thoughts of Melanie ebbed and flowed, now the memory of the day her seven-year-old daughter died was crystal clear. Millie walked slowly up the stairs, through the screened-in porch, front room, and dining room, steadying her gait on chairs strategically placed to prevent a fall, a fear that haunted her.

In the kitchen, she leaned against the counter and took in a big breath before tugging hard on the fridge door. The door, usually stuck, opened without a whimper throwing her a bit off balance. She was prepared for its unpredictability and had braced herself against the counter and widened her stance. The ice build-up around its freezer compartment required another forceful tug.

Standing over the sink, she turned the tap and watched the water filter down between the cubes till the glass was full. She felt the cold water slide down her throat. The ache in her chest subsided. The memory of that long-ago day was as clear to her as the cool water's refreshment was to her dry mouth. She walked with the glass into the dining room and sat down on one of the matching chairs at the large oval table. The table and chairs, together with a hutch on one side and brimming bookcases on the other, left barely enough space to walk through the room. An old frayed-at-the-edges lace cloth covered the table's surface and hung halfway to the carpet below. Plates, cups, and saucers, arranged in neat stacks, covered half the table. The hutch stood waiting for the dishes to find their place beside collections of old teacups, platters, and mementos already in residence behind its glass doors.

Millie, engulfed in her memories, glanced at the dishes on the table without seeing. She was in her second-floor Chicago apartment, with the window wide open, collecting a bit of breeze on a hot summer day. She heard the screech of tires, the car door slam, and a loud scream. Then, "Oh No!" She scanned the room to see where Melanie was. Her hand came to her throat, just as it had that day long ago. She leaned out the window and caught sight of the pink tennis shoe of the small figure lying on the ground. She stumbled down the stairs and ran into the middle of the street and knelt beside a sobbing girl. The girl covered her face with her hands and leaned on Millie's shoulder, moaning, "Oh, God tell me she's not dead! Please, tell me she's not dead."

Millie felt afresh, the nausea rising in her stomach as she bent to place Melanie's head in her lap. She recalled the ugly gash on Melanie's forehead and saw the blood from the wound seep into her skirt as her daughter gave one last gasp and was still. Memories of the rest of that day she could never recover. Nothing beyond the moment when her child lay heavy and lifeless in her lap.

Her co-workers filled her in on all the details later. Said the teenage driver had called the ambulance and waited with Millie till it arrived. Millie had stood silent with tears streaming down her face as the medics lifted the body from her lap and carried it to the ambulance. No siren. Her co-workers told her she had ridden in the back of the ambulance with her daughter, but Millie remembered only the lifeless body in her lap.

Millie's tears stopped. The deep ache in her chest diminished and she sat down to rest. Her eyes drifted to the large volumes on the bottom shelf of the bookcase. The letters on their two-inch spines were still legible despite their age. *The Wonderful Wizard of Oz, The Emerald City, The Tin Woodsman, The Cowardly Lion...* a series of seven altogether. Their bright colors had faded over time, and they begged to be dusted. She bought them more than 50 years ago, five days before the accident.

A vision of her daughter with the exact same pose as the little girl across the street and a plea of "There's nothing to do, Mommy," had prompted Millie to take her daughter shopping. Melanie discovered the Oz books on a shelf in the store, arranged at just the right height to tempt a young child. They cost more than Millie wanted to spend. She couldn't resist the "Please, Mommy, please," recited over and over as she tried to pull her away from the bookshelf. Millie talked the supervisor into a payment plan which allowed her to take the books home that day. They planned to start reading them together after supper, the day of the accident.

She sighed and bent to pick up one of the volumes. Her back reminded her of the reason so much dust had collected. Taking in a deep breath, she emptied the glass and rose. "Well, the lawn has to be mowed," she said aloud. She opened the screen door and looked across the street. The stoop was empty. She looked down toward her unfinished mowing and noticed the child leaning on the fence. She looked up at Millie, "Can I help you mow the lawn?"

Millie smiled slowly, opened the gate, and held out her hand. The child drew back. Millie dropped her hand and opened the gate wider.

"Come on in the yard, child." Millie stepped aside to let her pass. "What's your name?"

"I'm Jenny," was the almost inaudible answer.

"I know you haven't lived here long. I wondered what your name might be. Gracious, it's hot out here. It's much cooler in the house. Come inside, I'd like to show you something."

Jenny followed, glancing back across the street as Millie opened the screen door.

"It's okay, Jenny, I'll let your mother know I invited you in." Jenny smiled and trailed Millie up the steps to the screened-in porch, through the front door with the scratchy oval glass in the center, across the spacious living room, and into the cramped dining room. The dusty staleness made Jenny's nose crinkle. Her eyes struggled to adjust to the dim light inside. She looked up at crowded clusters of small ceramic figures on narrow corner shelves. Millie noticed and took one down, dusted it with her sleeve, and handed it to Jenny. Jenny sneezed as she reached for it. She slid her hands over the smooth ceramic glaze of the figurine. She looked closely at the ceramic doll and the hat on its head.

"It's a nurse. It's so pretty. When I grow up, I'm going to be a nurse," she announced, handing it back to Millie.

Millie returned the doll to its place and pointed to the big bookcase. "Jenny, see the books on the bottom shelf there. Can you dust them off for me? My old back won't let me lean over that far." She handed Jenny a tattered cloth. While Jenny dusted, Millie watched the dust particles become airborne and reflect the sun streaming through the side window. Jenny read the names of the titles: "*The Tin Woodsman, The Cooowaarrdleee Lion.*" She sounded out each one as she finished dusting it.

"How old are you, Jenny?"

"I'm eight. I'll be in third grade next year! Do the books have pictures?"

"Yes, lots of pictures."

Jenny tugged on *The Wonderful Wizard of Oz*, pulled it off the shelf and it fell over on its side. She drew the bulky volume onto her cross-legs and let it open into the lap of her dress. She fingered the gritty stiff pages. She paused at bright colored sketches of munchkins, monkeys, and the tin woodman. "The paper looks like newspaper, but it's thick and the letters are bigger," she said." You can borrow the book. When you finish, bring it back and you can borrow the next one."

Getting to her feet, Jenny managed to pick up the *Wonderful Wizard of* Oz. She brought it to her chest and walked slowly across the room. Millie held doors open for her as she passed through the house and stood watching as Jenny first stopped and looked both ways before crossing the street. Jenny's mother was standing outside her front door and waved at Millie as Jenny disappeared inside.

* * *

Thus, began the summer, with Millie delighting in watching Jenny come skipping across the street. Jenny's presence fostered in Millie an ebb and flow of sorrows. The sorrow began to soften. Memories of good times she had with her daughter came bubbling up when Jenny laughed. A pattern of warmer memories of her daughter became tightly woven together with the day of the accident.

Millie was startled the first time she heard her own laughter, dormant over so many years. She had come here to be alone. The old house had given her the sense of peace she craved and eased the pain of dreams lost. Yet with Jenny, there came a fresh measure of contentment. She heard her own laughter mingled with the child's. She treasured the feel of Jenny's small body leaning against hers. Millie brought out other books lingering on the dusty shelves of the bookcase. They were books Millie read with Melanie before the Oz books were purchased. She enjoyed Jenny's pleasure as they took turns reading aloud to one another.

Toward summer's end, Millie was sitting on her front porch swing and looked up to see Jenny slowly walking across the street hugging the last of the big volumes to her chest. A car approached, saw Jenny, and braked. Millie, hand at her throat, closed her eyes. Hearing nothing, her eyes opened. The car had stopped in time. Jenny hadn't even looked up.

Still shaken, she noticed Jenny's usual smile was gone. Jenny frowned as she climbed the porch steps with the big book. Millie held the door open. Jenny walked into the dining room. Millie followed behind. Kneeling on the floor, Jenny wedged the big book back onto its place on the shelf and let her fingers run across the backs of all the thick volumes. "I read them all, Miss Millie." Her usual smile returned as she closed her hand around the fingers of the hand Millie offered. "When I get old, I will have a big gray house. I'll let my hair grow long and find a lawn mower to push, just like yours."

Millie felt her throat tighten. No words came. What escaped was something between a laugh and a sob. Her hand tightened around Melanie's. They walked out to the porch and settled into the gentle rock of the swing.

MAGGIE AND MR. CHARLES

MAGGIE LEFT HOME and walked out to the edge of town. The sun was hot on her shoulders. She felt the sweat on her forehead when she brushed her red curls out of her eyes. She hated the way the sun made her freckles stand out. Her mother's voice still rang in her ears, telling her how to behave, the best route to walk to the boarding home, on and on and on. Maggie quit listening long before her mother finished. She knew where the boarding home was. She'd seen it out the school bus window as she rode back and forth to junior high school.

When Mrs. Murphy called yesterday and asked if she could work there weekdays, Maggie had almost dropped the phone receiver. "Yes, yes!" she'd said before Mrs. Murphy got to the second sentence. A bit of babysitting and ironing for neighbors was all she'd been paid to do past summers. She was glad Mrs. Murphy didn't ask her more questions on the phone, only said. "Well then, come to work tomorrow around noon. You can help with lunch. Then you'll need to be here eight to four Mondays through Fridays. No weekends."

"Does she know I'm only 14? Who told her my name was Margaret?" she asked herself.

The gate in the white picket fence stood open, its hinges so rusty she couldn't make it close. Tops of the fence slats were worn through to a dull gray. A cracked uneven sidewalk led across the middle of the spacious yard leading up to the house. Dandelions bloomed in abundance with patches of grass tucked in between. She liked the bright yellow tops, and the way they changed into a puffy lace she could blow off and watch float away.

She looked up at the three-story tall house and tilted her head back to view its eaves and gables off the third floor. She almost lost her balance when her sneaker toe caught on tufts of grass sticking up between the sidewalk cracks. She looked around hoping no one else had seen her trip, then watched her feet more carefully as she walked.

Round metal tables and chairs were strewn across the lawn, a few already occupied by men eating lunch. She noticed one table had a plate of food on it, but no chairs. As she approached the house, she could see its peeling paint. It reminded her of helping her Dad scrape off old paint from their house and picket fence and apply fresh new paint. Her nose crinkled as she recalled the sharp smells of new paint. Maybe she'd get to help make the old house and fence look like new again as a part of her job. Mrs. Murphy hadn't explained much on the phone, just said she needed help.

Maggie climbed the steps, walked across the open porch, and reached up to knock. The door swung open before her knuckles made contact. She looked up at the gray-haired woman staring down at her through the screen door. She must have been watching me come up, she thought.

"You're small, Margaret. Guess you'll have to do. Can't get anybody who wants to work here."

Mrs. Murphy pointed toward a man in a chair near the front steps. "That's Mr. Charles. I want you to help him to the table over there." She pointed to the table with no chairs Maggie had noticed before.

"He can't see, Margaret, so make sure he doesn't fall."

Mrs. Murphy shut the inner door before Maggie could ask what to do after she got Mr. Charles to the table. She shrugged, turned, saw Mr. Charles start to rise from his chair, and called to him as she walked quickly down the stairs.

"Hi Mr. Charles, I'm Margaret. I'm going to help you get over to the table for your lunch."

"Yeah, yeah, I know, I heard. I got ears."

She reached out and grabbed his arm to help him stand straighter.

"Take your hands off me!" he yelled. "You'll knock me over." Startled, she dropped her hand and stepped back. He sank back into the chair. She wasn't sure what to do next.

"Sorry, it's my first day," she said. "Tell me how I can help you get over to the table."

"Stand over here on the right side by my chair. Now put your left hand across your waist. Let me find the crook of your arm."

He waved his right hand around in the air. Maggie took his thin skeletal-like hand and placed it on the back of her left upper arm just above the crook. His hand surprisingly gripped hard. She struggled to remain stable as he pulled himself up. When standing, his upper body bent slightly forward so he stood shorter than she'd expected.

She handed him his cane, then moved forward slowly. He walked by her side and slightly behind moving his cane back and forth across the bumpy lawn. When they got to the table, his body brushed against it, and he dropped his cane on the ground to free his hand and grab the table's edge. His bony fingers tightened around her arm pinching her skin. His body weight almost pulled her over. She planted her feet and stood firm, glad he couldn't see her wince. He slowly unwound his fingers from her arm, so both hands now rested on the table as he leaned forward to support himself. She picked up his cane and hung it over the edge of the table.

"Just give me a minute, Margaret, to get my balance. Where's the chair?"

"There isn't one at this table, Mr. Charles. I have to find one."

"I can stand here by myself. Go find a chair. Get one for yourself too and sit down and talk to me while I eat."

Margaret dragged a chair over from a nearby table and brought it up to the back of his legs. "Push it in a little further. Then I'll be close enough." She pushed the chair forward as he lowered himself into it, found a chair for herself, and sat down across from him. She felt awkward now. Couldn't think up anything to say. She was relieved when he started to speak.

"Call me Charlie, Margaret, that's what everyone calls me here. Behind my back they call me the grouch. They think cause I can't see, I can't hear either. I don't mind. It makes 'em leave me be."

"Okay. You can call me Maggie. I told you Margaret because Mom said I should use my formal name so Mrs. Murphy would think I was older. But I like Maggie."

"Well, if you call me Charlie, I'll call you Maggie." She remembered hearing her mother say, "Now you be respectful." Maggie knew that meant no calling adults by their first names.

Charlie began feeling around the edges of his plate and touching the food.

"Are you going to eat with your fingers, Mr. Charles, I mean Charlie?"

Charlie laughed, "No. Just trying to find the food on my plate. Sometimes I can tell what it is by touching it. I'm not sure about everything. Here's what you do, Maggie. Pretend the plate is a clock, tell me what each food is by where it is on the clock."

"Beans at two o'clock, piece of chicken at 6 o'clock, potato at 9 o'clock," Maggie said.

Charlie found his fork and spoon and began eating.

"You are so clever, Mr. Charles, I mean Charlie. I would never have thought of the clock thing." He smiled. "Well, Maggie. I'm glad you know how to stand still. That Francis who worked here last summer wiggled so much I fell over twice and had to tell old Murphy to keep her away from me. I was lucky I didn't break a leg."

The silence stretched out. She was again unsure what more to say. She heard her mother's voice in her head. "Now don't go asking too many questions. Just do your work." Her mom knew she liked to chatter. Charlie interrupted her thoughts.

"Maggie, you still there?"

"Yes, Charlie."

"You got so quiet. Thought you'd gone off somewhere. Let me tell you bout this place. I'll give you the scoop, so you'll be of some use around here."

Maggie giggled. Charlie's loud gruff explosive laugh startled her. Men at tables nearby looked over at them. She could feel her face redden. Charlie seemed to sense it and lowered his voice. He said, "Mrs. Murphy isn't much for words, but she'll treat you fair." He told her about what Mrs. Murphy would ask her to do and about the other men who lived there. When he asked about her family, Maggie told him how her older brother called her freckles and what a pest her younger sister was. She told him her mom worked in the town fruit plant. "I think Mom must have told Mrs. Murphy about me wanting to be a nurse or something. How else would she have known my name? I think my mom knows she doesn't have enough money to send me to nursing school, so I am glad to get to work here. Dad works out of town, so I don't see him much," she said.

"How come you live here, Charlie?" He told her "I lost my wife, almost ten years back. My vision got worse after she died. Now all I see is blackness. I couldn't keep up our old house and wanted to get away from the memories. Old Murphy came over to my place one day. Told me a friend of hers told her I might be interested in living here. Didn't like the idea at first but - the best decision I ever made. It might look run down here to you, but it makes me feel right at home. My old place was falling apart too, but now it's not mine to worry about." Maggie didn't want the conversation to end, but Charlie had finished eating and pushed his chair back.

"Maggie, this is going to be a great summer!" She knew he couldn't see her smile, so she said. "For me too, Charlie. Thanks for giving me the scoop."

The summer slipped by. Maggie helped with laundry and getting the meals and Mrs. Murphy gave her lots of time to be with the men. "Go keep them out of my hair," she'd say. On Maggie's last day at summer's end, Mrs. Murphy told her "Don't know what I'll do without you." Maggie asked if she could work a few hours a week during the school year, but Mrs. Murphy said. "No, that wouldn't do. Maybe next summer."

She saw Charlie sitting in his usual spot by the porch as she came down the steps and went over to say goodbye. "It was a good summer, just like you said it would be Charlie." She touched the back of his long fingers. He turned his hand over to hold her hand and squeezed it. "Now Maggie, you come back next summer."

Maggie walked through the rusty gate, and looked back once over her shoulder, Charlie waved at her, and she waved back. She headed toward home kicking rocks off the toes of her sneakers as she went.

There was no next summer. Maggie's mother said they had to move at the end of the school year. Her father had found a better job in another town. Maggie walked over to the old house the day before they were to leave hoping she'd find Charlie to say goodbye. She was startled to see the old house with boards on all the windows. When Maggie got home, she asked her mom if she knew what happened to the boarding home, but her mom said she'd heard nothing about it.

As the family drove by the boarding home on their way out of town, Maggie glanced out the window. Thoughts surfaced in her mind. 'Why didn't I notice the house being boarded up when the school bus passed by? Why didn't I visit Charlie after last summer? Wish I could have said goodbye. Guess I thought I'd be working there again for this summer for sure.'

There was too much chatter in the car about the place they were moving to for Maggie to stay inside her head. She joined in with her sister and brother peppering their mom and Dad with questions about where they were going, what the house would be like, and the trip ahead.

*****

Now 80 years of age, Margaret stood in her kitchen finishing the breakfast dishes at the sink when her cell phone rang. Margaret had dropped her younger name Maggie when her family moved long ago. She'd told her mom, "Margaret makes me feel more grown up."

Margaret dried her hands on the dish towel. Probably another one of those scam calls, she thought, but the number looked familiar. She touched the phone's green circle and said Hello. It was a woman she'd met at the senior center where Margaret volunteered.

"It's Janine, Margaret, I need you to help me out, hope you can." Janine was talking fast.

"You know, I've been the group leader of the Low Vision Group at the Senior Center. It meets tomorrow at 11. Anyway, my daughter had an accident. I have to fly out tomorrow to be with her and take care of my grandson. I know it's last minute, but I hate to cancel it. Could you do it? I thought of you because you told me you used to be a geriatric nurse."

Janine stopped talking. Waited for an answer.

"Margaret, Margaret, are you there? Are you there?"

"Yes, Janine, I'm here. Had to think a minute. Yes... yes, I'll do it."

"Oh, thank you, thank you so much, Margaret. I didn't know where to turn. The staff sets up the room and gets everyone seated. All you gotta do is keep 'em talking. Gotta go, gotta get packed."

When Margaret entered the room where the group met, she counted ten men and women already seated, five on each side of the long rectangular table. Three walkers were propped against the far wall. Two chairs were still empty. A man with a cane was headed toward one. Margaret headed for the remaining chair, sat down, and waited for the man with the cane to be seated. She took a deep breath. She told them her name and explained why

Janine was not there and then a bit about herself.

"I was a geriatric nurse before I retired. Always liked being with old people. Now I'm old myself, and I still like old people," she said.

She heard a couple chuckles and relaxed. She hadn't led a group in years, wasn't sure how it would go. She continued.

"To get to know you, it would help me if you'd each tell me how well you see, and then why you're here today. Who'd like to begin?"

The man with the cane, said, "I see nothing, no light even, just blackness. Been that way the last three years."

A woman named Gloria said, "I only see blurred forms, odd shapes. Sometimes things seem to disappear, then reappear. It is strange."

Only three in the group said they saw well enough to read, but glasses didn't help. Each of them described a different type of magnifier that worked for them. No one's vision was the same. Of the three who saw nothing, one said it was all black, another said she saw light but no forms, and a third said "The light and dark vary. It doesn't seem to matter what time of day it is. My doctor can't tell me why it does that."

The room was quiet after everyone finished. She felt it had gone well and saw there were still fifteen minutes left to fill. She was thinking about what to say next, when the man across the table who'd said he only saw blackness asked, "Well, how about you? Are you blind?"

"No, I can see well," Margaret said. "Have to put glasses on to see the fine print. Don't need them otherwise." She recalled Janine was almost blind and felt the group was likely disappointed to hear she had good sight.

She paused... and it seemed Charlie was in the empty chair next to her. She smiled. "But let me tell you about someone who taught me a lot about being blind." And she told them about the long-ago summer. Her heart walked her back to sitting across the table from Charlie. She felt 14 years old again. She told them about how he'd taught her to take his arm and help him find his food. The group laughed when she told them how startled she was when Mr. Charles yelled at her when she pulled on his arm. Her voice tapered off as she finished telling them how sad she was to see the house boarded up.

Then the man who'd shared how he'd become blind in just the past year told the group about the struggle it had been to find his way around. "Yeah, I always gotta be tellin' people what it's like to be blind. They haven't got a clue!" Gloria added, "Yeah, guess they need to learn it from us." There was laughter all around the table and Margaret noticed heads nodding in agreement.

Margaret looked at the time on her cell phone. "Well, time to go," she said. "Janine told me they have to clear this room out at noon sharp for the next group." Chairs scraped the floor, and members of the group with some vision helped those who had none. The man with the cane, who'd come in last, was also the last to leave. He was feeling round the chair for his cane. Margaret found it for him. As soon as she put it in his hand, he waved her aside.

"I can manage now, Margaret. That's all you have to do."

She stepped back out of his way and went to make sure the door was open wide enough for him to pass through. The room now empty, Margaret slowly closed the door behind her as she left and whispered into the air. "Thank you, Charlie."

CANDLE

What? Write About a Word?
"Pick a single word" Keith Eisner, our writing instructor said.
"See where it will take you." I choose a word

       A candle lights two empty plates in a darkened cafe
     prisms of flickering light
     reflect in empty wine glasses

  A couple sits
    the waiter comes
    one chooses,
    other says, I'll have the same
    menus gone

  A basket of rolls set on table
    hands reach in basket
    fingertips brush
    hands entwine across the table
    knees touch underneath
    eyes meet

Each alone in their own world
 yet together
    breathe in the pleasure of other
    see candle flames dance in other's eyes
    longing to be ... more intimate
    closer, skin on skin

Transported beyond words, sight, and sound
    heads lean closer
    fingers caress palms of other
     lips smile

The waiter arrives
    bodies lean back, fingers untwine
    wine is poured, food set at table
     eyes lower
    hands reach for wine glass stem
    fingers pick up spoons to taste warm soup
    murmured *delicious* hangs in the air

 Silence descends
    to savor the food while still warm?
    no… to be done before the mood extinguishes
    to move beyond here
    to different dimensions of deliciousness

Now eighty years of age, amid my writing class, so unexpected when I began, how *Candle,* a single word, brings me to feel again *delicious* pleasures of my youth.

BARBARA MOULD YOUNG

Stories Through Time

DEPOIS DA HORS DO URUBU
(After the Hour of the Vulture)

1967

THE EVENING PASSEIO of arm in arm young women parading by the young men spending time together in the *parque* watching the young women, has ended. The vulture completed circling. The guitars put away. The town bedded for the night, and children are falling asleep. A single light bulb hangs from wood rafters in the main rooms of simple homes burning bright against the darkening night.

With long auburn hair, Cassy stands in the frame of the back door of her clay-floored home, alone, looking out beyond the well to the backyard garden. The well is now silent from the day's gossip of neighbors around its rim. Evening is settling from an active day. The night is quiet. Except... Ever so faintly, Cassy hears distant chanting, reminiscent of a religious service, yet different from the organ Bach cantata she would hear at home.

A small gentle wave of the day's released heat wafts across the dark, bringing in its mist, enchanting rhythm. She listens intently as if the beat is coordinating with her heart and is calling to her through the darkness of the night. She hears it signaling, as a beacon, Come, join the song, and dance to the enticing beat.

Stepping forward into the night in the direction of the sound, Cassy leaves the security of her home and her Midwestern caution for whatever lies before her. As if a rope is tethered around her waist, pulled toward the sound in the night. With just enough light to illuminate her steps and keep her from stumbling, she follows the road by the light shining around the cracks of doors and windows of houses huddled close to each other and just a step off her path. Her pace unites with drumbeats. She is tugged forward into the darkness.

Cassy is not aware of how far she walked when she reaches a large meeting house on the edge of the *sertão*, the scrubby backland. On the front door is a carved wooden mask of *Oxací*, the God of Travel. She shudders, feels chills over her body even though the night is hot. The beat in her brain urges her to grab the handle, take the risk and discover what is on the other side. Shaking, her hand pushes against the door. It opens to movement, music, song, and dance. She slides onto a bench in the back of the room. Her senses acclimate to the scene. She gets her bearings and tries to blend in even though her skin color is pale compared to theirs.

Two bare-chested men in rolled-up pant legs engage in an athletic dance of cartwheels toward each other as if wanting to kick a foot to the head of the other, then backing off, not touching, but threatening. Cassy witnesses the ancient dance of *capoeira*, amazed at the men's athleticism and energy.

Black-skinned women's bare feet tap the ground with the same beat as the drum. Their white billowing dresses scrape the dirt floor. Like waves of the ocean, the women undulate, stretch their erect bodies. Heads held high. Eyes look to the thatched roof. The pose holds for only a second. Then women bend low, as if trying to touch their heads to the floor. A cacophony of voices matches the undulations.

Entrancing music focuses Cassy's attention on the band. Five men in short-sleeved shirts and khaki shorts, with toes in flip-flops, create the sound that drew her to this place. Two drummers beat on cone-shaped drums and one man plays the bottom of a large metal oil can. Three more men form a string section, strum *berimbau* which blends a twangy pluck. With a small metal stick, another man clanks against a metal double horn-shaped instrument. Metal against metal adds a two-toned tinny accompaniment.

These musicians and dancers are descendants of enslaved ancestors who came from Africa to work in fields of sugar cane in Bahia on Brazil's eastern coast. The sounds they make come from their souls, as part of their DNA. Arms of the drummers and faces of the undulating dancers glisten with sweat.

The *Mãe de Santo* (Mother of Saints) begins to shout, swirl, shake, scream words from an ancient language – *"Eminotim vê, É, ê, ê, Andó xó cá ê vô a, A, a!* Her eyes roll back. In a trance, she is possessed, connected with the Spirits. Dancers back away and give her the space to undulate. After four minutes of possession, the *Mãe de Santo* crumbles to the ground, exhausted. Dancers assist her from the floor and attend her as others catch the spirit, shaking and shouting.

A hand reaches over to Cassy and offers her a smoke, an invitation to join the celebration, move from spectator to participant. She takes a deep puff, passes it back, and lets her muscles and attitude relax. The hand returns, offering a cup. She accepts and drinks an unknown juice called *juremí*. No longer chilled, Cassy eases into the environment. Her bones absorb the music. Intoxicated, the twang of the berimbau, and the beat of the drums, urges her to join the dance.

Having drunk from the cup, Cassy rises from the bench and moves forward into the dancing. The Spirits possess her. She is now the one undulating, swaying back and forth, swinging side to side, singing, *"Eu sou Amerinho. Su sou vista pena. Eu sou vim en terra para beber juremí."* (I am a little American. I only wear feathers. I come down to earth to drink juremí.). Cassy shouts and shakes, sweats, and glistens. She dances until her muscles relax, and she falls to the hard-packed ground.

Cassy, the young Peace Corps Volunteer from the heartland, reared in the Gothic Presbyterian Church, the dedicated nurse who once wore a starched white nurse's cap laundered to cardboard stiffness by the Chinese laundry, tonight let go of her proper persona, joined the Spirits in dance, and experienced ecstasy. Tonight, Cassy became a part of the community she came to serve. She is *Dona Americana* and *Dona Branco*. Affectionately, she is now *Minha Neguinha,* my Little Negra.

Dancers of the Condomblé Barbara Young 10/1/22

EMILY AND ALFAHAD

1990

IN THE CENTER of the corral, twelve-year-old Emily plunks herself down in the tall grass, out of sight. Her half Arabian, half-quarter horse grazes nearby. "It's tough, Alfie. I don't fit. I don't have friends like the other kids. They say, 'You're weird.' Then they pal up and ignore me. I'm not invited to birthday parties. It hurts to be left out. It's lonely at school. You listen and understand. Here, I can let the breeze rustle the grass, and it smells like wheat. I can touch the tassels, and they feel silky. It is as if the wind talks to me…and understands. I hear the birds. They speak to me… Alfie, come here. Let's go for a ride."

Emily climbs up on a stump and pulls her horse close. She intertwines the fingers of her left hand into Alfahad's wiry black mane and her right hand around his strong velvety neck. Emily lifts her right leg over and pulls herself onto his back. She feels the warmth of his body and the inhalation of his breathing. Her knees grip tightly, and she adjusts to a balanced riding position. With understanding each other, they exit the corral for the road.

As horse and rider meander through the rural neighborhood where the expansive lawns yawn toward the ditch at the side of the road, Emily rides past the house on stilts, land that floods when Cypress Creek overflows. Past the lawyer's house with the swimming pool where neighborhood kids gather on a muggy day. Past the park of the gas line company bordered by a high chain-length fence. Past the community water tank deep among the trees where Grandma Susan wandered lost in the middle of the night, the sheriff retrieved her. Past the Snyder house where stately columns pretend to be a southern plantation. Past the Lynch family retreat from the Borough of the Bronx. Past the Burris family home with a truck of ten tires that totes five kids everywhere. Past the Travis' who loan their Toyota truck so mom can pick up Alfie's hay and alfalfa bales. Past the house with the mean dogs who decimated the chicken stock and made no reparations. Emily knew this neighborhood, each inch and lot of it. Alfahad swishes his long tail swatting annoying flies.

A crow family gathered in a nearby tree and chattered among themselves. "The crows are smart," Emily tells Alfahad. "They know who I am." Emily listens, engaged in her environment, glad to share her thoughts with Alfahad.

Emily's parents are getting a divorce. Her mother is barely coping and doesn't want to talk. Emily feels she couldn't share her confusion and pain with anyone at school. Her mom tells her they will have to sell Alfahad and had placed an ad in the local newspaper – "Horse for Sale."

A large horse van pulls up in front of their home, the tail ramp unlocks, and lets down to the asphalt road. A confident domineering woman dressed in her western best walks from the street to the front door. Emily, alone in the corral with Alfahad speaks to her horse, "Alfi, I don't want you to go; you are my best friend." She wraps her arms around his neck, leans her face into his warm brown skin, and breathes in his horsey smell. "That lady can't love you the way I do. She doesn't seem nice. Oh, Alfie," and cries into his warmth.

The buyer is pleased with Alfahad's pedigree. Emily overhears the lady bragging about her new silver saddle, and she doesn't have the money for the horse just then. The lady walks toward the corral. "May I have the lead for your horse?" Saying nothing and turning away from the buyer, Emily allowed the tears to fall freely.

Alfahad is led from the corral, down the drive, up the ramp, and into the van. The ramp lifts, and the door locks. The horse trailer moves slowly down the street, turns at the corner, and is soon out of sight. Emily remains hidden in the tall grass long after the horse van pulls away.

Emily is told to start packing. Her turquoise leather jodhpurs, the ones she wore in the western class competition and won first place, are given to the boy next door. The house is sold. She and her mom are moving west.

Grandma's pin cushion with Emily's signature

PURPLE RUFFLES #ME TOO

1985

"EVERYONE KNOWS BUT YOU."

I had my head bowed over my mother's seventy-year-old featherweight Singer Sewing Machine, pushed five yards of purple netting under the pressure foot, and gathered the fabric into an elastic waistband. The gown would be worn for my daughter's high school band's formal dance. Old Singer hummed along at an experienced worker's pace. I focused on holding the fabric to the half-inch marker. Speaking with increased intensity and purpose, Suellen directed her words to me in my prayerful position.

"Everyone knows but you," she repeated.

I paused. The presser foot stopped in the up position. Suellen was silent, waiting. What didn't I know? The mortgage was up to date. The horse was not sick with colic. Freddie was still employed. My part-time school nurse job was intact. I didn't like playing this guessing game. Could not my daughter provide details instead of innuendo? Yet, I felt in her words an intense pain, something primal activating my maternal instincts. It took my breath away. I felt fear in my gut. I had to face that what I had hoped for so long was not true.

My mind flashed to a visit to the Florida Everglades last year when the nature guide told us that after baby alligators were hatched, mother alligators kept watch for an entire year to protect them from the father who would eat the young as fresh, moving food. I thought of the sacred relationship of spouses and the protective care of the young they share. I keenly felt my daughter's words ripping my soul.

"Everyone knows but you," she said for the third time.

"Do you mean…?"

"Yes, he got my sister, too—when she was little, shortly after you married him. We tried to tell you four years ago when we lived in Richmond. You didn't believe us then, so we didn't talk about it after that. Kept it to ourselves, until now. Audrey and I want you to believe us."

"Yes, I remember you tried to talk to me. I couldn't understand and did not want to believe it; I shut down, so I didn't have to think about it. It was too awful. I didn't ask questions, avoid the subject, and tuck the conversation away as if it did not happen."

"He has not abused us since we moved to Texas three years ago, but Emily is now the age of Audrey when he first abused her. We want you to protect Emily.

"What should I do?" I asked.

"I don't know," Suellen answered.

"What can I do?"

"I don't know," she answered again.

I sat in silence, for what seemed an eternity. Then I heard the back door open downstairs. Freddie was home. Only then did I leave Suellen's room.

"Freddie, you have abused the girls."

"Barbara, I would not do that. I love the girls, all three." Freddie was adamant in his denial. He reversed the accusation as if I were imagining the disclosure. He minimized the topic for discussion, accused me of fantasizing. His manner of speaking and words were strong, rehearsed, convincing. Messages in my mind were jumbled. I began to prepare our dinner as if I were working remotely. In the days that followed, I felt kicked in the stomach and couldn't breathe. Suellen's words reverberated in my brain. I encouraged the family to go with me to family counseling.

"No," said the girls.

"Yes," said Freddie.

Where do I turn for help? I had a good relationship with Emily's grade school counselor, Ms. Green. She had helped Emily to adjust to the concept of an open classroom when Emily needed structure. She had counseled when Emily acted out inappropriately and called a team conference when Emily struck the principal, her authority figure. Picking up the phone, I dialed Counselor Green. "I can recommend Mr. Todd, the assistant minister of the local Methodist Church, she said."

We had been attending the services at the Methodist Church. I was unaware of this assistant minister, but I accepted Ms. Green's recommendation and called for a family counseling appointment.

The church conference room had one chair on the end of a rectangular table where the counselor sat. Freddie and I sat facing each other on opposite sides of the table. We formed a triangle. For a church classroom, this room was notably devoid of pictures of Jesus helping little children. No Bible psalms on the wall. No vases filled with artificial flowers or palm fronds.

Mr. Todd looked like an official clergyman in a dark suit jacket, white shirt open at the neck as if trying to be casual. He was youthful and his clean-shaven face was clear of blemishes. He had heavy black eyebrows against a pale face. I would lose him in a white man line-up. Mr. Todd explained how he would conduct the counseling session. He would open the session with us both together to understand the issue between us. Then he would see each of us separately, in what he called an individual caucus. After caucus time, the three of us would reconvene for a closure. Freddie and I agreed to this format.

I spoke first. "My daughters have revealed Freddie sexually abused them. Emily, the youngest sister, is at the age now when the abuse began, soon after I married Freddie."

Mr. Todd turned to Freddie. "How do you respond?"

"I did not abuse them. The girls miss their father. I try to be a good stepfather, and I certainly do not want them to forget their father. We have moved further away, which makes it difficult for their father to see them."

Time for a caucus. Freddie left the room leaving me alone with Mr. Todd. I began explaining that my oldest daughter, now age fifteen, revealed Freddie's sexual abuse began when she was seven and for her sister, age five. The abuse with the two older girls continued after the move to Richmond but has not continued since the move to Texas. I do not know if Freddie has abused our daughter Emily, but she's had disciplinary problems at school, including assaulting the principal. Emily is taking Ritalin for Attention Deficit Disorder, ADD, which the school nurse supervises. She is picked up by the special needs bus and transported to another school for class in behavior modification.

The minister counselor was quiet through my disclosure, saying little and not asking questions. Freddie and I switched places, and I took a seat in the hallway three classroom doors from the conference room. I sat on a vinyl-covered loveseat facing the wall with pictures one would expect to see in the Methodist Church. One was a picture of the head of Jesus with long brownish-red hair, his kind eyes looking up as if in wonder of the heavens. Another was a scene of John the Baptist and Jesus gathering at the river for baptism. A third was of Jesus dressed in a long flowing white robe, sitting on a rock, surrounded by small children who looked up to him. A small stand, supporting a large vase of artificial red geraniums, was set under the Jesus and children painting.

When Freddie's private session was over, Mr. Todd summoned me back for the closing conference. I had no idea what Freddie had discussed with Mr. Todd, but I was surprised to feel that I was the one excluded, on the outs, as if I had been the accused party and what I had disclosed had no validity. Mr. Todd began. "Freddie thinks you are a saint and speaks well of your work at home and with the school district. He told me about your move to Texas and how you set up home here."

The closing session was that—closure. No discussion came from our separate sessions. The minister might have interviewed the girls separately, but he made no mention of doing so. Nor did Mr. Todd suggest another session for Freddie and me. He left me hanging as if my revelation was a fantasy and the abuse did not happen. Session ended.

As I left the pale-faced minister in the bland conference room, it felt colder than when I entered. My daughters had put their trust in me to speak. Was domestic violence not a subject one could discuss? Could there be a conspiracy of secrecy? Why is it that when I finally broached the subject and had the courage to put it on the table, I was the intruder into the club? I did not know what to do next or whom to believe or whom to trust with my disclosure. If the Methodist minister did not believe me, whom could I trust? Family members returned to work, school, activities, and the issue of sexual abuse was hidden, yet it remained a festering blister in my brain. I was again floating above the earth looking for grounding.

DREAM TIME: "HERE LIES SON OF A BITCH"

1990

I AWOKE with a startle. Breathing hard, I looked around my bedroom with its familiar blinds, the window half open to let in the summer night air, and the mirror on the wall. I knew where I was. I had had a dream, a strange one. Within the dream, women's voices spoke of a foggy history. When I calmed down, I recalled the fine detail of the dream. I allowed my head to sink back into the grove of the pillow, continuing the drama where it had paused.

Five women surround his casket, gaze with malice at the well-dressed stiff, and express their venom at the now silent body.

"*Son-of-a bitch*" says a statuesque blond-haired woman, with a long coat over her scrubs, wearing white nursing shoes. "I met him when he came into the hospital with a heart attack. He was dead, but the attendants revived him. I have a large family in Northern Kentucky and with all his smartness, he was lonely and wanted family. We moved in together and had a son born at the same hospital. I didn't trust him with my child and left our son with Grandmother Annie while I looked for independence to get away from him.

"*Filho da Puta,*" says an attractive Black woman with a medium build and short-cropped tightly curled hair, dressed in a colorful full-flowing skirt, puffed-sleeve blouse, brown leather sandals. "I was a poor immigrant from the *nordeste do Brasil*. I was his *empregada* - his housekeeper, laundry woman, and cook, plus all the 'extra' services he demanded. I needed income and he took advantage of it. He was the dominant white male and I, a poor Black immigrant, his sexual slave."

"*Son-of-a bitch*" repeats an athletic, short, red-haired woman in brown oxfords, an earth-mother type. "He told me his first wife was dead, and his second wife was living the drug scene in California. I believed him. Among us middle-class folk looking for an interesting date at the Methodist Church, he made a respectable image, a successful businessman on the rise. It was when he picked up his precious young son from the nursery that I visualized being the loving stepmother the child needed. He told me he wanted dependents for a tax break and wooed me with red roses, Godiva Chocolates, and singing Italian love arias. I fell for his Big Lies."

"*Hijo de quejarse*," says the last voice raising her arms as if dancing a Flamenco. She was tall, well attired in a stylish red-print wrap-around that highlighted her black hair and brown eyes. Her stylish high heels augmented her five' eight" height. "My late husband and I were in business and had our own hacienda in Cuba. Castro took over and confiscated our estate. We immigrated to America. When my husband died, I became a widow with a disabled son. When I met this man at the Methodist Church in Houston, I believed his lie of being an executive for an environmental engineering company. I had fiduciary responsibility for North and South American holdings for a large estate. When Freddie proposed, I thought my life would be full of music, have an intelligent helpmate, and fill my lonely hours. Instead, he hacked my business account and abused my mentally retarded son."

"*Son-of-a-bitch,*" repeats a soft-spoken attractive greyed-hair retired librarian. "Widowed, I thought I had met a man who needed me. Told me his wife had died of cancer. I empathized with his grief. I fell for his charm, stories, and beautiful Irish tenor voice. Only later did I realize he loved my home as a calm hiding place for his identity."

These five women were weaving a bond in empathy, securely, as if a shoelace were crisscrossed back and forth across the body of the deceased. Looking up at each other, the women smiled in appreciation of who they were and in anticipation of what was yet to come. They chuckled and adjourned to the tavern next door.

FULLY RESTED, I awoke late the next morning, laughing and lying-in bed savoring the visuals of the dream. Was the dream about Freddie? What would be the number of interesting women in Freddie's life? Would a gaggle of women come to his funeral? What were the stories they would share? Were they as naive as I? Did they believe the Big Lies?

PRAYERS

2014

LOOKING at the monitor, I saw an X-ray of the skull and spine with a grey spot, the offending tumor. My daughter Emily's life flashed before me: birth in Cincinnati, moving on her first birthday to Virginia, growing up among the azaleas, and rhododendron, and loving to climb the dogwoods, moving west to enter kindergarten in Texas, and learning to ride and own a horse. When I divorced her father, the two of us moved again, and she entered junior high school in Washington State. The neurosurgeon was explaining his procedure, speaking to me, the terrified mother:

"You can see on the monitor the tumor is at the base of the skull. We will use a laser beam with pinpoint accuracy to cauterize the tumor. My surgical team will make a helmet for Emily which will secure her head to the surgical table. She will be unable to move her head."

Surgery of the brain and spinal column frightened me, and I had to trust the competence of the neurosurgeon and recent technology that made this surgical procedure possible. Emily's brain power was not shabby. For two years, the Capital High School Academic Decathlon team represented Washington State in a national competition. Emily won Honorable Mention in the national competition in mathematics. After taking all the science courses offered at the community college, she went on to graduate from Washington State University with a bachelor's degree in Genetics and Cell Biology. I was proud of her accomplishments and respectful of her abilities.

The technician heated a piece of mesh plastic sheet and

molded it to Emily's face with a connecting sheet wrapped around the back of her head. The mask molded to her unique features and contour and screwed into place, making her immobile for the laser trajectory focused upon the offending tumor. This procedure was quite different from the ancient brain surgery - inserting a stylus into the brain to allow evil spirits to exit. After surgery, Emily gave me the two pieces of the plastic shield, serving as a model to study in the ceramic studio. I built healing masks, prayers kneaded into the clay to form a shield against illness, and prayers offered for Emily's complete recovery.

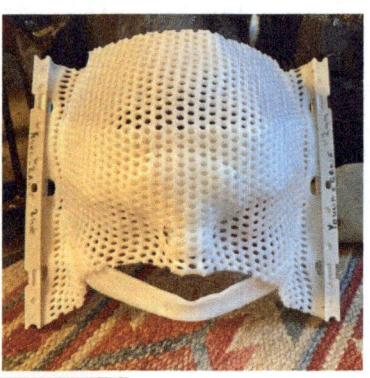

Shield & Masks

LET

THE DAY AFTER *the Presidential election November 9, 2016, our writing teacher Keith Eisner gave us the prompt "Let."*

Let me be accepting…as
The political vote
Did not go in my favor

Let the new leader learn to compromise
Soften his tongue
With those of different faces

Let me recommit to those values
That made our country
The hope of those who came searching

Let me roll up my sleeves
Retreat to a quiet room
Use my pen to speak truth

Let me love with confidence
Sing with harmony
Dance for freedom

Let me live
The precious life
I have been given

BEETHOVEN, CHOPIN, JOPLIN

2016

I LOVE THESE GUYS. I took private lessons on piano and violin from fourth to eighth grade. Entering high school, I shelved the music and focused on cheerleading and Latin. At age seventy and retired, I returned to music lessons and listen to what the composers are communicating, letting me know their moods through the notes, tone, and spacing. Centuries may distance us, but their music brings us together.

Beethoven is egotistical, elegant, effusive, creative, and brilliant. He is complicated and composes no notes the same. It is a pleasure to collaborate with him, to decipher what it is he is proposing. His music is impressive, and it is a challenge to play what he has written. It takes me months to figure it out. Each time I play, I discover something new. When I play correctly, I know he is pleased. To be coordinated with Beethoven's genius with my fingers touching the piano keys is communication through the keys.

Frederick Chopin is a romantic. I want to pull up my long full skirt like Ginger Rogers and dance around the room with my partner's hand on my back guiding me in step with the music. Bodies touching, we swing and move across the dance floor falling in love all over again. My piano teacher said I am waltzing too intently and do not put my hands together in the right way. I'll keep practicing.

Joplin has a syncopated rhythm, unlike any other composer. A steady left-hand moves back and forth over the keyboard.

The right-hand fits its melody in between the chording of the left. Remember *"The Entertainer"* from *The Sting* with Robert Redford and Paul Newman? It is Joplin's music. Learning Joplin's syncopation helps me feel I am playing piano in an earlier era.

Monday is lesson day. My teacher asks me to repeat two measures five times so that my fingers develop muscle memory and correct notes in the right order. I am playing Beethoven's *Moonlight Sonata*. Beethoven double sharped an F which means you are really playing a G, but it is not a G according to the signature; it is a double F sharp. Beethoven signifies this by placing an "X" in front of the double F sharp. In the same measure, I play another F which I thought was a single F sharp. It did not sound right and was not right because Beethoven expected me to be smart enough to know that unless otherwise marked, every F within the same measure would be a double F sharp. My teacher reaches for his green pencil and marks an "X" in front of the offending F. In the following measure, there is a single F sharp, so Beethoven has the courtesy to neutralize the preceding measure's double sharp by placing a natural sign and then a sharp sign in front of this F. But, this time, I guess correctly. I am learning to understand Ludwig's composing.

I am practicing *"Valse"* by Frederick Chopin. Instead of playing three hundred individual notes, my teacher encourages me to learn sequence, teaching my brain to think in groupings, bringing the burden of 300 to 100 note groups. In a note grouping where E is the base note and carried through four measures, my left-hand knows where to go and stays there.

In Scott Joplin's four-part *Swipsey,* I have the syncopation learned for sections one and two. In learning section three, I play the right and left hands separately, so each hand learns its own music. Then, I put the hands together and play three days without a pedal. The fourth day, I add the pedal to smooth transition, connecting the sections; yet, not overlapping. Once I learn section four and take the time to perfect the entire piece, I may be ready for Preservation Hall in New Orleans.

I love these guys.

DIA DE LOS MUERTOS
(Day of the Dead)

2019

Octobre 30

LAST NIGHT at dinner, we discussed Día de los Muertos, the celebration of the deceased ancestors returning to the living. The ancestors are welcomed back with food and drink. This October 30th is the two-year anniversary since the passing of my first husband Ken, father and grandfather to the daughter and children at the table. A place at the table is set for Ken. My son-in-law has prepared a fall squash, zucchini, and beef stew and serves it with pumpkin muffins. Granddaughter Nora retrieves a Dr. Pepper from the garage refrigerator and places it with her grandfather's photo before the empty chair at the dinner table. Stories of the family reunion with Ken in July 2017 to Yellowstone and the Tetons are shared.

When the 2017 Yellowstone family reunion is complete, Ken, his bicycle attached to the rear of the car and a heart defibrillator tucked into the passenger seat, drives his car away from the campsite for a solo adventure through the Southwest. After which, Ken drives north to Portland, Oregon, and east beyond Bend. Within a field of boy scouts and families camping, Ken joins daughter Katherine and the grandchildren for the total eclipse of the sun which passes on a direct path over Oregon. After the eclipse, Ken continues to drive east, returning to Ohio. On October 30, 2017, Ken serenely passes away from a heart attack.

Recalling these tender stories around the dinner table, tears flow freely, silently. As in the celebration of Día de los Muertos,

Ken's chair is occupied as we feel his presence. His spirit has returned to be with family for food and drink.

Octobre 31

AS I PLACE my pen on a white, lined, spiral bound three-holed writing pad, Grandson across the table opens his briefcase binder, removes his chrome book, clicks on "Translator," and begins his assignment for immersion Spanish. He glances at my effort with pen and paper. "How old-fashioned, Grandma." Liam and I exist on different clouds, different atmospheric spheres. With the computer lit up, I notice he picks up a pencil and applies his thinking to a white assignment sheet. We are back on the same planet.

Closing his briefcase binder and preparing for school, Liam leaves the house, cuts across the park lawn and into the woods. He boards the school bus on the next street. This evening is the official Halloween when children in costume take to the streets to visit neighbors. Nora will be a scary witch dressed in a sparkly black gown and a tall pointed hat. Liam will be a Patriot, or as neighbors interrupted – Hamilton, Washington, or John Adams. His ruffled white neck scarf, long sleeve tailcoat, and leggings with boots define each of these. The children use flashlights to walk in the dark to neighbors' houses.

LAST NIGHT the empty chair at the dinner table was occupied by the ancestor who had returned to join the family for food and drink. Tonight, flashlights light the paths of costumed children in the dark night. There is light enough to offer the deceased passage home.

FRIEND IN CARE HOME

Words

2021
July
"What shall we talk about today, I ask friend Mark
Nestled at his care home among the trees
"Words" he says. "We will speak of words.
Would you read one of my poems?" he asks

Pulling his notebook from bottom drawer,
I open to poetry, the first page
"This one is titled *Wall.* Shall I read it?"
Nodding "yes" his reply, I begin.

"*Walls……*"
Words of walls of his childhood
Of his home and being young
Distant, clear memories of long ago

"Read one of your poems," he requested
Page marked with a sticky note
I read of pelican diving for breakfast.
"Read another poem," he asked

Time passes quickly
Each sharing words of stories past
By the wall, by the sea
Distant, clear memories of long ago

Bidding good-bye
Close the poetry of our writings
Look forward to next week
A time to pause, exchange words

Words 2

<u>August</u>
In my absence of three weeks
Mark changed his residence care home
Compassionate caregivers immigrated from Kenya
Warmly greet me as their guest

"Mark teaches me English," Davis said
"And I teach him Swahili."
"A Fair trade," I note
As we knock on Mark's door.

Proud of his learning, Mark recites.
"Déo means 'yes'
Ha-pán-a is 'no.'
That's right, not reversed."

"Would you read my poem?" he asks
Pulling his notebook from bottom drawer,
Open to poetry, the second page.
I read his poem *Words.*

Opalescent, toothsome, blithe, bamboozled
The glowing of a gemstone
The radiant smile of a child
"Bamboozled is something I know firsthand."

Noticed field book on book stand
Amphibians and Reptiles, the title announced
"I was fascinated as a child,
and the wonder never left me."

Amphibians and Reptiles, words for today
Spoke of rocks, streams, walks, Swahili
Words of caregivers, current and past
sadness of illness, not knowing future

He hesitates, pauses a moment
searching for words that won't come
sees with eyes full of memories
"Sometimes, there are holes," he says

Words 3

September
Returning from sunny walk with Lois
Positions himself on bed pillows
Hands me his poetry notebook
"Pick one we haven't read," he asks

Open to poetry, third page and more
Slowly searching until I stop,
Fascinated, eyes focus on *Lost Dog*
Handing notebook to Mark, be begins

"Lost Dog, brown and white
Comes to 'Fluffy'
Doesn't bite
Big reward
"If you find her, beg her to return
Tell her that I've learned
This time I really mean it
Ask her to forgive me."

He looks up for my reaction
Sitting with tears in my eyes
Remembering pain of long ago
Lost dog was running from home

Visits become fewer, days less light
Words tucked away in poetry notebook
We pull now from bottom drawer
Read his words, treasure the stories

(Poetry of Wall, Words, Lost Dog are part of a published poetry collection of Mark Holland, Olympia artist, poet, and writer. Mark Holland died January 13, 2022 in Olympia, Washington)

CHRISTINE COLYAR

I was born in the summer of 1947 to an Italian mother and a Scotch-Irish father. My home has always been in Washington State. Since I was very young, I have been attracted to the storytelling of my Irish Grandmother. Her stories included traveling in a covered wagon and memories of the fabrics she stitched into the only quilt she made and gifted to me. Though I wondered about the connection to truth, I loved her tales and always begged for more. Her stories did add to my sense of self and place and my need to tell a story in search of who I am. My stories are a balance of truth and possibilities. They blend places where I have been and places where I yearn to be, the preciousness of family, and the challenges of distance.

I am a painter, poet, weaver, and short story writer. I write to find my place in the fusion of words that create my existence and to continue my beloved connections to my grandmother.

Welcome to a glimpse into my storytelling life.

BONNIE COTTON

Born in 1948, the youngest of four, babied and spoiled, according to my siblings. I wanted to be heard and seen, and stay out of trouble. I was raised among loving and accepting folk, within a safe farming community.

I married at 20 and was widowed at 24, losing the innocence of childhood and small-town America. I remarried, divorced, and married again while completing my college degree in Sociology, with a minor in religion. Full-time ministry was my vocation for 27 years. I loved the challenge of preaching, making the narratives of scripture and the teachings of the Christian Faith relevant and accessible to others; I accompanied many folk through their journey of birth, living life, finding love, experiencing transformational events, and accepting illness and death. I saw myself often as a midwife, awakening others to the goodness of ordered intention. I made my way in the world, determined to make it a better and safer place for my three children.

Widowed a second time, in retirement I decided it was time to turn family stories, my collection of letters and boxes of pictures, and my shelf of personal journals into a record of perseverance and survival, sharing my life lessons along the way. I write out of the roller coaster of joy and triumph, sadness and anger, loneliness, frustration, and extreme happiness that has been my life. I write to find the words to contain and acknowledge the impact of grief in my life. I write to process my experience for I believe love and loss are universal.

My current project is a Memoir of "Life with Bill: A Story Never Told," dedicated to my daughters.

JEAN COOK STICKNEY
---Jean Stickney Gant
---Jean Gant Delastrada

I was born in a blizzard in Newark, New Jersey, in 1947, the product of a "mixed marriage" – a Southern lady and the Yankee son of Slavic immigrants. From age 6 to 16 I lived in hot, stifling Texarkana, Arkansas. Ever since then, I've been trying to reconcile the differences, to make sense of the variations in people and their lives I've encountered.

As a teacher and therapist, I've been immersed in learning and in theories, leading to a focus on autism and schizophrenia. I've been writing a "personal and professional memoir" for almost twenty years now. I keep working and living and writing more stories. In this anthology, there are three of these stories, followed by my pandemic story, which takes me back to Texarkana—home?

DAN JORGENSEN

Born in 1951, Fresno, CA.

Moved to CA central coast at age 40 to work for Caldrons for 22 years, then retired, separated from a 39-year marriage, stopped drinking, stopped smoking, and moved to Olympia.

Residing in Olympia, WA since 2013 and married Celeste in 2017.

The reason I started writing: I started writing to entertain a friend, with an ongoing story. My writing was pathetic, the first story I'd written in two to three decades.

Favorite genre of reading: Magical Realism, entertainment via escapism. Fiction in general.

Hobbies: Volunteer handyman for Rebuilding Thurston County, making bellows, enjoying retired life with my wife and two-year-old Golden-doodle, reading, writing, walking, and cooking.

Careers: Calculator repairman, journeyman electrician, roadway inspector/electrician/materials/ compaction tester for California Division of Highways.

MARTHA ILES WORCESTER

Born in 1941, I turned eighty in 2021. I began writing classes at the Olympia Senior Center with Keith Eisner in 2015. My past career focused on nursing and teaching about older adults. My initial purpose in writing was to illuminate the lives of elders through creative non-fiction. It remains my primary purpose as the three vignettes included here illustrate. Along the way, I've found, I enjoy writing poetry and memoir. For my writing to be worth anything to anyone other than myself, I've learned it cannot be a solitary practice, but a group endeavor.

Acknowledgments to Keith Eisner, Our Writing Together Group, and Many Others

A special thanks to Keith Eisner who challenged me to write and taught us how to present our writing orally in public forums, and how to evaluate each other in clear and positive ways. He encouraged us, on graduating from his six classes, to launch our writing groups to sustain us.

Our Writing Together group has broadened my writing interests. The members' wide variety of approaches to writing and comments on my writing are a rich reservoir for learning and friendship. They share their homes and lives. Here is a bit of what I have received from each one.

- *Barbara Young spent hours on my booklet of poems* to give as gifts to my family in thanks for what they have given to me at my 80th birthday celebration. I never would have met the printing deadline without her. Sharing her personal stories leads me to share my own.

- *Bonnie Cotton shares so much of her own life experiences, marriages, and losses.* She enhances my ability to write about the personal. Her continuing joy and enthusiasm for life lessen my fear of the future should I lose my husband of many years.

- *Chris Colyar shares her artwork and crafts* with us. Her exquisite descriptions of nature expand my ability to describe the natural environment of my stories' settings. She often gives me just the right book containing writings like those I am trying to portray. So helpful!

- *Jean Gant Delastrada writes about* the spectrum of autism experienced by her clients and the families she serves. Her portraits of clients model sensitivity to those with difficult life experiences. She models for me how to do the same with characters in my stories.

- *Dan Jorgensen's sense of humor and caring* attitude shine through his prose-poetry about his mother, wife, dog, and carpentry projects. His fanciful fun fiction keeps us all laughing. His masterful editing keeps my writing concise, clear, and free of distracting errors.

- *Other helpful teachers have been Olivia Archibald and Jim Lynch.* Their rich bank of knowledge and time given to evaluating my writing encouraged me to continue.

- *Lastly, a heartfelt thanks to family and friends* who take the time to listen to my stories and provide both physical and personal space for me to do my writing.

BARBARA MOULD YOUNG

I WAS BORN in Dayton, Ohio in 1942, and as a four-year-old, worked in the family WWII victory garden of corn, tomatoes, and beans. My mother was reared on a farm in Pike County and was the first in her family to graduate college. She taught me gardening and nutrition. My father was born in Uxbridge, Canada, grew up in Niagara Falls, New York, and migrated to Ohio for education. He encouraged violin and piano lessons.

My right of passage at age twelve was a solo train trip to New York City to visit Aunt Lois and Uncle Irl in the Borough of Queens. I rode the subway, visited Carnegie Hall, and Wall Street, climbed to the crown of the Statue of Liberty, and viewed the city from the top of the Empire State Building. I experienced the culture of the city, the diversity of People, and the thrill of travel.

High schools in Dayton were segregated: Roosevelt for Black students; Julienne, Catholic girls; Chaminade, Catholic boys. We had three synagogues in our neighborhood. We shared observance of religious holidays. In 1964, the Civil Rights Act was passed, I graduated from The Ohio State University, and John Glenn flew into space. I married a college sweetheart, and inspired by President Kennedy, Ken and I joined Peace Corps as Volunteers in Brazil. Returning to the United States, we had two children. We divorced. I remarried, and after living with my second husband in Ohio, Virginia, and Texas, I left him in Houston and drove to the Pacific Northwest. I worked for the Washington State Department of Health, returned to school, and ran for Olympia City Council. In 1995, the Shoalwater Bay Tribe hired me. The Native women taught me to weave cedar baskets and construct masks for storytelling.

FLANNERY O'CONNOR said, "I write to discover what I know." Writing teacher Keith Eisner instructed us to write "wild pages" of whatever came into our consciousness without being edited and provided prompts to bring forth hidden stories of life experiences. I drafted stories of family, Peace Corps, and domestic violence. I wrote my first fiction with the encouragement of Jim Lynch, author of *The Highest Tide,* drafted a poem, and recorded visits with a friend. Through writing, I discovered what I knew - beauty, joy, and love.

Made in the USA
Monee, IL
13 February 2023

27280502R00095